MRS. MALLORY INVESTIGATES

MRS. MALLORY
INVESTIGATES

Hazel Holt

St. Martin's Press
New York

For Geoffrey

MRS. MALLORY INVESTIGATES. Copyright © 1989 by Hazel Holt. All rights reserved. Printed in the United States of America. No part of this book may be used or reproduced in any manner whatsoever without written permission except in the case of brief quotations embodied in critical articles or reviews. For information, address St. Martin's Press, 175 Fifth Avenue, New York, N.Y. 10010.

Library of Congress Cataloging-in-Publication Data

Holt, Hazel.
    Mrs. Mallory investigates / Hazel Holt.
        p.   cm.
    "A Thomas Dunne book."
    ISBN 0-312-03894-1
    I. Title.
PR6058.0473M77   1990
823'.914—dc20   89-27142
                                                CIP

First published in Great Britain by Macmillan London Limited under the title *Gone Away.*

First U.S. Edition

10 9 8 7 6 5 4 3 2 1

Chapter One

I must say, the first time I saw Lee Montgomery I didn't take to her at all. She was standing by the bar, buying another round of drinks for the men. Looking at her as she leaned against the counter, wearing one of those soft fawn suede jackets and beautifully cut trousers, I felt short, dull and provincial, although, until that moment, I'd been perfectly happy with my good Jaeger suit and my best (uncomfortable) shoes. I could see that Rosemary and Anthea weren't too keen on her either. They looked up from the murmured conversation they had been having and raised their eyebrows significantly as I came in.

My old friend Charles Richardson had rung me the evening before.

'Sheila, dear, I'm back in Taviscombe. Longing to see you. Can you manage a pub lunch tomorrow? I've asked Ronnie and Anthea and Jack and Rosemary – all the old crowd – and I specially want *you* to come. There's someone I want you to meet.'

'Who is it?' I asked.

'She's rather marvellous.'

All Charles's girl-friends were marvellous, so I didn't take much notice when he went on ('Looks fabulous . . . elegant . . . witty, vivacious . . .') until he mentioned the word marriage.

'She runs an estate agency here – the one that's selling Mother's house for me . . . marvellous business woman . . . I'm thinking of giving up my job in the States and coming home – I'll get some sort of consultancy over here . . . put some money into Lee's business . . . really want to settle down in Taviscombe . . . back to my roots, as they say . . . '

Charles and I had been at the local county school together – goodness, it must be well over thirty years ago – and so had the others. Except for Charles, we had all stayed in the small West Country town where we had grown up and had married locally, within our own little circle. But Charles had gone out into the world. He worked for one of those big multi-nationals and had lived in remote, exotic places, until he finally settled in America, married a girl from Texas and had two children. The marriage hadn't lasted, though, and Charles was soon back in the social swim of Cincinnati as an eligible bachelor. He kept me up to date with all his girl-friends, so much so that I really used to dread the sight of an American airmail stamp. I suppose I represented home, a fixed point in a shifting world, and, since I had been his first love in those far-off school days, I might be supposed to lend a sympathetic ear to his romantic entanglements. After his mother died about six months ago, he came back to Taviscombe to sell her house, but there were legal complications and he said he would be back soon. And here he was, talking about marriage.

I was curious, to say the least, to see the woman who had finally trapped – I found I used the word

6

instinctively – poor Charles. Anthea and Rosemary were saying 'poor Charles' too, as we sat in the pub waiting for the men to order the food, still hanging around Lee at the bar.

She came over and Charles introduced me.

'This is my dear Sheila,' he said, putting his arm around my shoulders, 'whom I've told you so much about.'

Her eyes flickered over us both and, obviously dismissing me as any kind of threat, she gave me a warm smile and held out her hand.

'Indeed he has,' she said. 'Never stops talking about you! His oldest friend!'

I smiled back, less warmly, making some colourless, conventional murmur.

As we drank our gin and tonics and ate our bar snacks, I looked at her more carefully. Seen close to, she was nearer forty than thirty. Her hair, I decided regretfully, was a natural ash blonde, thick and curly, and her eyes were a deep, unusual blue. She certainly looked marvellous and I could see why Charles was smitten. But still. She looks neurotic, I thought, watching her lighting yet another cigarette and tapping off non-existent ash with red-tipped fingers. She wore several rings, including a wedding ring. Charles said that she was divorced too, as if that somehow brought them closer together. Her manner towards him was comradely rather than loving – one of the chaps. Perhaps that was what he found intriguing.

When we all left the pub and walked through the car park, I wasn't really surprised to find that she drove a dark green Jaguar, not brand new, but obviously expensive.

'*Well*!' said Anthea, as they drove away. '*She's*

certainly got poor old Charles exactly where she wants him!'

'Just what he needs,' Jack said. 'Marvellous woman! Anyway, it'll be grand having Charles back here again.'

We contemplated this thought for a while.

'Yes, of course,' I said doubtfully, 'though, in a way, it's part of Charles's charm – being in faraway places.'

Rosemary laughed. 'Oh well,' she said. 'I'll believe it when I see it.'

Charles returned to America and life went on as usual. I found myself deeply involved in arrangements for our Christmas Fayre for Help the Aged and my thoughts revolved almost exclusively around lists of cake-makers and who was going to tell Miss Whittaker that she certainly *couldn't* run the children's Bran Tub after the mess she made of it last year. A middle-aged widow – I'm fifty-four actually – living in a small sea-side town must expect to be deeply involved in local activities. Taviscombe, indeed, is a town full of widows, but since I am younger and, relatively speaking, more mobile than most of them, I find that rather more is expected of me. When my husband died two years ago, well-meaning friends involved me in all sorts of voluntary work to 'take me out of myself', and since I was still quite dazed and numb after Peter's long illness and death, I simply did what was put in front of me, as it were, and after a while I found that they were right and that being busy did help.

Peter was a solicitor. Like me, he was born here and he was well-known in the town and had many friends, most of them people he had helped in some way, for he was a kind, generous and compassionate man. After he died I think that Rosemary and Anthea had some idea of *my* marrying Charles, but, fond as I had always been of him, I knew that it would never have worked. When you have known one really marvellous person everyone else seems second best, and I didn't want second best.

Then, of course, there is My Work, as my son Michael irreverently calls it. I write the occasional volume of literary criticism – mostly about the more obscure Victorian novelists – and am published by one of the university presses. Not many copies seem to get sold, but they do provoke an enjoyable amount of theory and counter-theory from other workers in the field, so that a good time is had by all those inhabitants of that esoteric little world of Lit. Crit. Very few people in Taviscombe have read my books, though several kind friends have ordered them from the library, but they have given me a little local fame and a defined place in our close-knit society: 'Sheila Malory is very *literary* of course, but quite useful on committees.'

In fact, I rather enjoy my Good Works: the Red Cross and Help the Aged, of course (who knows how soon one might want their help oneself?) as well as fêtes and jumble sales and coffee mornings for St Stephen's Restoration Fund, and Bring and Buy sales for the Friends of the Local Museum Association, not to mention the Archaeological Society and the Literary Society (where I am occasionally asked to give a short paper). And then, of course, there is Michael. Although he is nominally at Oxford, reading History, it seems to me that university terms are much shorter than they used to be, since he always seems to be at home requiring three large meals a day and constant laundry. It will be seen, then, that I lead what might be called a full life.

One morning just before Christmas I was standing outside Boots feeling rather annoyed. My car was being serviced and I had walked the mile into Taviscombe thinking that I didn't need much in the way of shopping – just a few odds and ends plus a quick visit to the bank and a long queue at the Post Office (oh the tyranny of the Christmas Card List). But I had been carried away by the glitter of Christmas decorations and, on impulse, had bought a large and ridiculously expensive box of crackers and other seasonal fripperies. Last year, after Peter's death, neither Michael nor I had felt much like celebrations, but this year I suddenly felt I'd like to make it really festive, with a tree, snapdragon and a Yule log if I could find one. Consequently I was loaded down with inconveniently shaped parcels and facing a tiresome walk. The last of the half-dozen taxis that were usually parked outside the market had been snapped up by a small but determined woman whose Yorkshire terrier had firmly wound its lead around my legs, immobilising me at a critical moment. The wind was bitingly cold and I wished I had worn a heavier coat. It might even be a white Christmas at this rate. As I stood there, wondering whether to wait for a taxi to return or start walking, I was aware that a car had drawn up beside me and someone was leaning across and opening the passenger door. It was Lee Montgomery in her green Jaguar.

'Hop in,' she said. 'I'll give you a lift.'

My first instinct was to refuse. I hadn't seen her again after Charles had gone back to America.

Well, that is not strictly true. I had, when shopping, glanced casually into the estate agent's window, peering round the photographs of Attractive Period Cottages and Charming Converted Coach-houses, trying to catch a glimpse of her. In the brightly lit interior I had seen her blonde head leaning forward as she persuasively spread out details of desirable residences for potential customers. A shadowy figure sat at another, lesser, desk in the corner, presumably doing the typing and general slave work. But we had not met face to face.

'Come on,' she urged. 'I'm holding up the traffic.'

I got in, rather flustered, tossing my packages into the back in such a hurry that I felt I had probably broken some of the more delicate Christmas Tree decorations. This made me feel even more churlish towards Lee until I pulled myself together and remembered my manners.

'Thank you. It was so good of you. It's absolutely *freezing* on that corner and there's no knowing when there'll be another taxi – I think they all go into hibernation in the winter!'

She laughed rather more than my feeble joke deserved, and I had the feeling that she wanted to placate me for some reason.

'Look,' she said suddenly. 'Are you in a great rush or anything? I mean, can you spare the time to come and have a drink before lunch?'

I must have hesitated a moment too long, because she added, 'Please, I want to talk to you about something. It's rather important. Well, it is to me. I'd be so grateful.'

I was immediately curious.

'Yes, of course. I'd like to very much. Won't you stop off and have a drink with *me*?'

11

'Well, actually, I've got to go up over the moor to collect some keys for a property. It's out towards Brendon and I said I'd be there by twelve-thirty – the caretaker can't wait after then. So if you wouldn't mind coming with me first, we could go on to the Stag Hunters at Brendon – they do quite good food there too.'

'That would be very nice,' I said rather formally.

As we drove she made no further reference to what she wanted to talk about. Instead she told me about her various property dealings – I had to admit that she was very amusing and her stories were vivid and funny. She seemed quite relaxed now. The moment of tension at the beginning of our conversation had gone and she was sitting easily, her hands resting lightly on the leather-bound steering wheel. She was wearing those driving gloves that have pieces cut out of the back – the sort worn by what I think of as Proper Drivers, who know about revs and double-declutching and nought to sixty in however many minutes it is.

'This is a beautiful car,' I said as we surged smoothly up Porlock Hill. I reached out and touched the walnut dashboard with my finger-tips. 'So elegant as well as so powerful.'

'I adore it!' she said, with such a sudden intensity that I turned to look at her in surprise. She gave a little laugh. 'It represents everything I wanted when I was young,' she explained. 'When I had absolutely nothing. It was the very first thing I bought when I finally got my hands on some money.' The phrase hung between us and she laughed again. 'Well, you know what I mean.'

We chatted amiably enough as we drove further into the heart of the moor. She was easy to talk to, though I couldn't quite bring myself to call her 'Lee', a rather affected, made-up name, I thought, presumably a more dashing form of a pedestrian one.

The sky was iron grey and the moorland on either side of us was raked by wind so that the scrub oaks seemed to be twisted and tormented as if possessed. The sheep huddled in what shelter they could find and a few ponies stood forlornly by a gate. There was very little traffic and the car swung round the bends of the road as if it, too, had a life and vitality of its own. We turned off the main road down towards Brendon, but instead of going down the hill she took a sharp turning to the right, along a steep, narrow lane, and then left at a farm gate.

'I don't think I've ever been this way before,' I said. 'Where does it lead to?'

'Oh, only the house. It's a dead end. Just the house and then open moor.'

We rounded a wind-break of beech trees and turned into a short drive. The house at the end was quite hidden from the road by a dip in the hill, but as we approached I saw that it was a large stone building, well-built and handsome, with stabling and several out-buildings. There was a lawn outside the front door and a quantity of rhododendron bushes and shrubs. I commented on them to my companion.

'They must look glorious when they're all in bloom. I don't suppose it's possible to grow very much in the way of flowers here, though I suppose you could have bulbs and various types of heather.'

'It's a very good property,' she said. 'Do you want to come and have a look or would you rather stay in the car? I won't be long.'

I love looking over houses so I said I'd come with her and got out of the car. The wind took me by surprise – it was miserably cold outside and I hurried after Lee towards the house. She didn't go to the front door, but went round the side, past the stable block, to what seemed to be the kitchen door. The back of the house was dark, overgrown with shrubs and trees right up to the back door.

'A bit gloomy,' I said. 'I imagine all this was servants' quarters – I suppose it didn't matter about *them* having any light. But I suppose there aren't any servants now. Difficult to get anyone to stay this far out – unless they're horsy and want free stabling in return for a little light domestic work.'

We went into the kitchen, which was large and seemed very bleak and empty. The desolation was emphasised by a few abandoned saucepans and kitchen utensils. There was certainly a lot of modernisation to be done before this could be described as 'desirable', I thought. I followed Lee along a passage and out into the main body of the house. It had obviously been a hunting lodge in the days when such places were built on Exmoor for the stag-hunting season. The rooms were very Edwardian, elegant and spacious, with high ceilings and handsome fittings on the panelled doors. The wallpaper was patched with damp and the cold struck us in the face as we entered the drawing room.

The caretaker obviously felt the cold too, since he was anxious to hand over the keys and be off. We heard him drive away and Lee said, 'Come on, we'll freeze to death here. Let's go and have a warming G and T.'

As we drove away I looked back at the house.

'Goodness,' I said, 'you can't tell there is a house there at all – it's quite hidden by the hollow ground and the trees. Does it have a name?'

'It's called Plover's Barrow – after the farm in *Lorna Doone* I think. Anyway, it sounds good.'

We were both glad to get to the Stag Hunters Inn. There were very few people there so we were able to sit right on top of the log fire and thaw out.

'It really is a handsome house,' I said. 'It could look marvellous if you had it done up. Though it might be difficult to find someone who wanted to be so isolated – it must be all of five miles from any other house and ten miles from the village.'

'I hope to get a deal on it,' she said, 'a really good deal. That house is going to make me quite a lot of money. Certainly enough to buy me an absolutely smashing trousseau from Jean Muir. Yes,' she smiled, 'that was what I wanted to talk to you about. I'm going to marry Charles.'

'Congratulations,' I said rather stiffly. 'I hope you will both be very happy.' I tried not to let my doubts about the likelihood of this show in my voice.

'I know you don't approve,' she said. 'None of you. You all think I'm marrying Charles for his money.'

I didn't say anything and she went on, 'Well, in a way I am – at least, the money will be jolly useful. The firm's cash-flow is what you might call static at the moment. Things are in a bit of a mess and, quite honestly, I need Charles's experience as well as his money to help me out of a sticky situation. But that's not the only thing. I can't say I'm madly in love with him or anything like that, but I like him a lot and I'm quite happy to settle for that.

15

I'll make him a good wife, you know.' She looked at me seriously, her deep blue eyes very dark. Then she laughed. 'We'll have a lot of fun. I know Charles likes a good time, and he'll enjoy having someone to spend all that money on. Anyway, it's time he settled down. But the fact that he wants to settle down in Taviscombe makes it important that you, especially, should be on our side, should approve, go on being his friend.'

'Oh well,' I said, 'I don't think my opinion would be that important to Charles.'

'Oh yes it would. You mean a lot to him. I was almost jealous of you.' We both smiled, knowing precisely how her jealousy had evaporated when she had actually seen me. 'I want it all to be just right. I want to settle down too.'

For a while I didn't say anything. There didn't seem to be much that I could honestly say. I still felt that Charles deserved more than just liking from a wife, but perhaps he would never really know exactly how Lee felt about him. Like so many men he was perceptive only when it suited him, finding it easier to tuck unpleasant truths away and see only what he wanted to see about human relationships, which was odd, since he was immensely shrewd in business and had an eagle eye for any imperfection in a commercial contract. One of the logs fell on to the hearth and startled me.

'Thank you for being so frank with me,' I said. 'I hope it all works out.' I could see that she had noticed my change of phrase. 'When are you going to be married?'

'We haven't quite decided. I'm going over to Cincinnati for Christmas and we'll discuss every-thing then.' She pushed her half-finished steak and kidney pie to one side of the plate. 'Do you want coffee?'

'Well, actually, I think I ought to be getting back. I don't like to leave my old dog for too long – we both like to have a little walk in the afternoon and it gets dark so early now,' I added, thinking how dreary and elderly I sounded.

'Of course.' She stood up and pulled on her driving gloves as I gathered up my bag and scarf. 'Thank you for listening to me.'

As she walked in front of me to the car, I envied her her strength and vitality and her sureness about what she wanted from life. But I didn't envy her possession of Charles. In a strange way, in spite of myself, I wished her well.

Christmas came and went, with its customary pleasures and pains. Michael went back to Oxford and I somehow got through those first miserable weeks of the New Year when it seems that everything has died for ever. I had a large, jolly, very American Christmas card from Charles, and a note, just after Christmas, to say that Lee's visit had been a tremendous success and that she had met his two young sons and they had all got on wonderfully together. So it seemed that everything was going to turn out to the satisfaction of all concerned.

One night towards the end of January I had stayed up late, much later than I usually do, to watch an 'open-ended discussion' on Channel 4, which had gone on until well after midnight. I had just fed Tristan, my little dog, and was engaged in the usual chase around the house to catch my Siamese cat, Foss, to put him in his basket, when the phone rang.

'Sheila?'

It was Charles, and I wished, not for the first time, that he could keep track of the time difference between our two countries.

'Charles!' I said insincerely. 'How lovely!'

'Sheila,' and now I noticed that his voice was strained and anxious, 'you've got to help me. Lee's disappeared!'

Chapter Two

For several moments I couldn't think what Charles was talking about. From the kitchen I could hear furious Siamese howls which meant that Foss had stopped thundering up and down stairs and was waiting for his supper.

'Disappeared?' I repeated stupidly.

'Yes. She went back to Taviscombe after Christmas and rang to say she'd got back safely and that she'd phone in a few days to finalise the wedding arrangements we'd made when she was in Cincinnati. And then nothing. For nearly three weeks I've been writing and phoning, but she hasn't replied to my letters and no one answers the phone in her flat. And when I ring the office I only get that stupid girl who does the typing, and all *she* says is that Lee is out of the office on business and she can't reach her. It's like banging my head against a brick wall! *Please*, Sheila, will you go and see if you can find out what the hell is going on? I'm absolutely desperate.'

'Well, of course I will. There must be some perfectly ordinary explanation,' I said. My mind doesn't function very well late at night and I couldn't really take in all the implications of what Charles was saying. 'Don't you worry,' I said in a calming tone.

'I'm sure it's all perfectly simple.' I was aware that I was repeating myself but there didn't seem anything else to say. 'I'm sure it's all right really.'

'You'll let me know immediately you find out anything?'

'Yes, of course I will.' I was repeating myself again, but I was so tired I couldn't think of any other words. 'I'll go into the agency tomorrow, first thing.'

A circular sort of conversation then took place, with Charles repeating how worried he was and me trying – rather incoherently – to reassure him. After about five minutes of this I said firmly, 'This must be costing you a fortune – I'll let you know what I can find out. Goodnight Charles, take care of yourself,' and put down the phone.

In a sort of daze I fed Foss, automatically tidied the sitting room and went wearily up to bed. Needless to say, as soon as I had washed my face and brushed my teeth I felt wide awake and my mind started churning over Charles's extraordinary story. What on earth could have happened? Had Lee had second thoughts about marrying him? But I was sure she was not the sort of woman to evade an issue. She would certainly have faced Charles and told him outright that she had changed her mind. I didn't imagine that she cared over-much about hurting people's feelings. But why? It was obvious that she needed the money, and marriage to Charles would be a perfectly agreeable way of getting it. I hit my pillow vigorously, then sat up, put on the light and had a drink of water. The problem remained insoluble and I had a sleepless night.

The next morning I found myself inventing household tasks that had to be done – little bits of washing, cooking the animals' fish, repotting a rose geranium – anything to put off the moment when I had to go and see what I could find out. I was uneasy about the whole affair and reluctant to get involved. Bother Charles, I thought.

I approached the estate agent – it was called Country Houses – cautiously. Studying a photograph of a Character Country Cottage, Needs Some Improvement, I tried to peer into the interior, but because of the reflections on the glass I couldn't see anything. There was nothing for it but to go in.

There was no sign of Lee and the place looked rather run-down and desolate. A girl was sitting at a desk with her back to me, sorting through some mail. As she heard me come in she turned, and to my surprise I recognised her.

'Good gracious, Carol! I didn't know you worked here!'

'Mrs Malory!' She seemed equally surprised to see me. 'Don't say you want to sell that lovely house of yours!'

Carol Baker was a girl you couldn't help admiring. She had married young – far too young, I suppose – and her husband, Derek, a worthless layabout Peter used to call him, had been in and out of trouble for years. They had two small children, and when Carol was seven months pregnant with the third, Derek had gone off to London and never been seen since. I imagine he lived precariously on the fringes of the criminal world. She had come to consult Peter about tracing him and getting some sort of maintenance for the children, but he had drawn a blank. Still, Carol was cheerful and hard-working and was managing to bring up the children splendidly. We had both taken to her

21

and tried to help her in various little ways – Peter
sorted out her DHSS problems and I passed on
various items for the children that I picked up in
the course of my sale of work and jumble sale cir-
cuit. Carol was, I think, grateful for Peter's efforts
on her behalf (she wrote me a very touching little
note when he died) and always seemed pleased to
see me. But not this morning. In fact, she looked
rather disconcerted.

'Did you want to see Mrs Montgomery?'

'Yes. Isn't she here?'

'No.' Carol hesitated. 'I'm afraid she's away on
business at the moment.' She sounded as if she was
repeating a formula rather than stating a fact.

'Oh,' I said casually. 'When will she be back?'

'I don't know really. Is it about a house?'

'No, Carol. I've come in because Mr Richardson
– you know, her fiancé in America – is very worried
about her. It seems that he hasn't heard from her for
nearly three weeks.'

'Yes,' she said rather flatly. 'He has phoned several
times.'

'But don't you know where she is? She must
have said something.'

'No, I don't know.'

Her face was expressionless, unlike the Carol
I knew who was normally very lively.

'Oh come *on*, Carol, she can't have just gone
off – all that time ago – and simply said nothing!'

'No, she didn't say where she was going.'

'Poor Mr Richardson is terribly worried,' I said.
'They're getting married soon – he can't understand
it. Surely you must know something. You know you
can trust me.'

She hesitated, and then took a deep breath and

said, 'No – I must tell someone and I know you won't let me down.'

I drew up a chair and sat down beside her at the desk. 'No, of course I won't. Tell me all about it.'

'Well, when Mrs Montgomery came back from America she was all excited and yet sort of nervy, if you know what I mean. She smoked all the time and whenever the phone went she wouldn't let me answer it but always snatched it up herself. Well, after about a week, she told me that she was going away for a few days on business. She seemed ever so keyed up about it so I thought it must be something very important. She said that she didn't want anyone at all to know she was going to be away – especially Mr Richardson. She repeated it several times – you know that brusque way she has of talking – she could be quite frightening sometimes. Well – what could I do? He kept ringing and asking me about her. I had to keep putting him off.'

She sat hunched up, her hands gripping the edge of her desk.

'I felt really mean, not being able to tell him anything when he sounded so upset, but Mrs Montgomery was so insistent ... She's not an easy person to work for at the best of times and you know how difficult it is to find any sort of job in Taviscombe, and I need the money for the children ...'

Her voice trailed off again and she looked at me despairingly. I gave her what I hoped was a reassuring smile.

'It's all right, Carol. Of course I won't let Mrs Montgomery know that you told me anything. But it *is* very odd, you must admit. Do you have any idea at all of where she might have gone?'

Carol hesitated. 'Well, there was something. The day before she went away she had this phone call. It was at lunch-time. I'd gone out to do a bit of shopping and it started to rain, so I had to come back for my umbrella and she was on the phone. She had her back to the door so she didn't see me come in, and I heard her say, "Very well then, Jay, I'll meet you half-way. Wringcliff Bay – that lay-by on the left coming from you. At twelve o'clock. You'd better make it this time, or else— " And then, when I came up to my desk to get the umbrella, she saw me and put her hand over the phone and said, "What the hell are *you* doing here, creeping about like that?" She was really angry so I just said I was sorry and took my umbrella and went away quickly. When I got back after lunch she was nice as pie and said she was sorry she'd snapped at me but I'd startled her. I sort of felt that she was trying to pass the whole thing off, make out it wasn't important. But it was, I'm sure.'

'Jay?' I said questioningly. 'You don't happen to know who that might be?'

'No. I've never heard her mention anyone of that name – it's quite unusual, isn't it, I'm sure I'd have remembered.'

We both sat silently for a while. I felt Carol relax, as if she had transferred some of her problems to me – trustingly, as she used to do with Peter when he was sorting things out for her. Almost as if she expected *me* to sort out this particular problem now that Peter was no longer here. I felt a kind of responsibility to her now, as well as to Charles.

'Carol,' I said briskly, 'let's try and get all this straight in our minds. When did Mrs Montgomery go away?'

24

'Tuesday, January the third. It's a very slack time with us, just after Christmas, so I suppose she didn't worry about leaving me to look after the office for a bit – though I'm sure she didn't mean it to be this long.'

'Right. What about her appointments?'

Carol went over to the larger desk and took an engagement diary from the drawer. 'There isn't much here, because it's a new one. There's nothing down for Tuesday the third. Look.' She brought the book over to me and we examined it.

As Carol had said, it was a new diary and the only entry in it was for the following day, Wednesday 4 January – just two initials: 'P.B.'

'You don't happen to know who P.B. is?' I asked Carol.

She shook her head. 'No – she must have made the appointment when I was out of the office.'

We seemed no further forward, but I tried to sound reassuring.

'Don't you worry, Carol. I'll ask around, talk to her friends and see what I can find out. If we don't get any news soon, though, we may have to tell the police.'

'Oh no!' Carol was really agitated now. 'She'd never forgive me if I did that!'

'But Carol! If she's disappeared we really ought to inform someone in authority – I don't think she has any relations and you must admit that it's very strange.'

She shook her head. 'No, no, you mustn't. There might be things she wouldn't want the police to know about, and she'd surely give me the sack if they came poking about here!'

'What sort of things?'

'I don't know exactly, but I got the feeling, sometimes, she was doing things that weren't quite right. I don't know enough about business to know what it was – it's just a feeling. But you do see that I daren't call the police . . . '

'It's all right, Carol. Don't worry. I'll see what I can find out myself. We'll leave it like that. I promise not to go to the police just yet. Cheer up – it'll be all right.'

I picked up my shopping basket. 'How are the children? I suppose Brenda's at school as well now – goodness, how the time flies, I can hardly keep track!'

I chatted away soothingly about the children and she seemed calmer when I left her. But now I was the one who felt agitated.

Outside Country Houses I looked at my watch and realised that I should have been at the St John's Ambulance headquarters twenty minutes ago to help set up the stalls for the Bring and Buy sale for the Stroke Club. Rosemary wouldn't mind but I could expect sarcastic comments from Marjorie Fraser, the rather difficult woman who was running it.

As I had expected, she greeted me with a bleak smile.

'I'm so glad you could come after all, I was afraid you might be too busy – I know how *many* commitments you have.' That was a dig at me because I had been elected to the Ladies' Luncheon Committee and she hadn't. 'Rosemary and I have put up nearly all the trestle tables. Of course it *is* easier with three, but we managed.'

Rosemary pushed her hair back with a rather

grimy hand and said, 'Oh, it was okay. They're not really heavy – just very dusty. Who used them last? Was it the Scouts? I do think someone might have wiped them down!'

I apologised profusely and took the other end of the table Rosemary was manhandling. Marjorie Fraser took herself away to boss another group of helpers who had just come in with cakes and jam and potted plants.

'*More* marmalade!' I heard her say. 'Oh well, I suppose *someone* will buy it!'

Rosemary giggled. 'It really is a bit much. The wretched woman hasn't been in the town for five minutes and she's running everything in sight!'

Marjorie Fraser was another relatively young and active widow with time on her hands. She had come from somewhere just outside Bristol where her husband had been a vet. I don't know how long he had been dead – in fact I didn't know a great deal about her. She never volunteered information and I didn't like her enough to find out. She had taken a house, in a village outside Taviscombe, with a paddock and stables for her two horses. She was one of those tiresomely horsy people who despise everyone who is not equally fanatical. She hunted twice a week in the season and all the time she could spare from doing whatever one has to do to horses she devoted to running things. Quite a lot of people disliked her but were glad that she was prepared to take on the more tiresome tasks, even if they resented her way of going about them. She was a tall, angular woman with a brisk manner, and Rosemary and I avoided her whenever we could.

We put up the rest of the tables and Rosemary said conspiratorially, 'Come on, while she's not

27

looking, let's escape and go to the George for a pub lunch.'

We washed the dust off our hands in the cloak-room, and as we slipped out we could hear Marjorie Fraser's voice relentlessly going on, 'It would be most unsuitable to have *instant* coffee. And anyway, if we have really *good* coffee we will be able to charge twice as much . . .'

We made our escape.

The George used to be a very splendid Edwardian hotel set in pleasant grounds near the sea. Nowadays, in the summer, it is fairly intolerable, with wooden picnic benches outside which attract a lot of young people with motor-bikes and old cars, but in the winter it can be quite pleasant, if one goes into the Lounge bar.

We hurried past the Saloon bar, raucous with juke-box and fruit-machines, full of young people, mostly those who stay behind after the end of the season, living on social security in winter-let bed-sitters, waiting for summer jobs again. There seemed to be more of them than ever this year, and as we settled ourselves in a peaceful window-seat in the Lounge bar, Rosemary commented on how unpleasant it had become in the town, to see them hanging about in noisy groups, even jostling the frail and elderly off the pavements.

'What are you going to have?' she asked.

'Just a toasted sandwich for me and a glass of white wine.'

Rosemary ordered our food at the bar and returned with two glasses.

'They're bringing the toasted sandwiches when they're done,' she said. 'I got you ham and cheese.'

We made those little fluttering noises and protests

that all women seem to make when they are settling up any small sum of money, and then Rosemary said, 'Did you have a good Christmas? I haven't really had a chance to ask you, what with Marjorie Fraser banging on all morning. Did you hear from Charles? We had a Christmas card but it didn't say anything much, only love. Did that Lee woman go over there?'

I wasn't sure if Charles wanted me to tell anyone else about Lee's disappearance, and, honestly, devoted as I am to Rosemary, she is the last person I would ever trust with a secret, so I simply said, 'Yes, she did, and it all seemed to go marvellously well.'

Rosemary snorted. 'Well, if Charles can't see that she's only after his money . . . Men!'

I laughed, and Rosemary plunged on into other subjects.

'Can you come and have drinks on Sunday? Jilly's coming for the day with her bloke.'

'Jilly's bloke' was Rosemary's attempt at being modern and nonchalant about her daughter Jilly and the boy-friend she was living with in Taunton. He was a nice young man, from what Rosemary had told me, a police inspector, and there seemed to be no reason why they shouldn't have got married in what to me was still the normal way. But, as Rosemary explained carefully, as one repeating a lesson, they felt they wanted a more open relationship.

'Actually,' Rosemary said, sounding slightly guilty, 'Mother's coming too. Of course, she wants to see Jilly, but you know how she feels about her and Roger – not that she's met him yet. It's that generation, I suppose. *Anyway*, she's so fond of you, so if you *could* bring yourself to come and take her mind off things, as it were . . . '

I said that I would be delighted.

'Oh, bless you! See you on Sunday then, about twelve.'

I went back home and got out the ironing board. A lot of people hate ironing, but I find it very soothing and conducive to thought. I like the feel of the iron sliding over the material, and the way the creases are magically smoothed away. My thoughts ranged over what Carol had told me. Where *was* Lee? Presumably she had gone to meet Jay, whoever he (she, even, people had unisex names nowadays) was. Had she returned from that meeting or had she gone off somewhere with him? And – my thoughts became circular – where was she now?

Foss suddenly materialised, as he always did when I was ironing, and jumped on to the ironing board, seeking the warm spot where the iron had been. I addressed him as if he could solve my problem.

'What on earth should I do, Foss? There's nothing much I can tell Charles. I suppose *he* will have to be the one to go to the police if she doesn't turn up, after all he's her fiancé – more or less. But then, if there's some perfectly simple explanation, she would be absolutely furious.'

Foss gave a loud wail and lashed his tail across the board in front of the iron.

'I know,' I said, 'I can go round to her flat. There might be some sort of clue there.'

There was another loud wail, possibly of affirmation. I opened a tin of cat food and put some down for him so that I could have my ironing board to myself again and finish my task. Then I made myself a cup of tea, and as I drank it I

30

looked at the telephone directory and found that Lee lived in a block of flats by the sea-front. Definitely desirable and expensive, which meant that they would be guarded by an entry-phone. Fortunately, though, an old friend of my mother's also lived there, so if I went to see her I could at least get inside the building.

'No time like the present,' I told Foss, and picked up the telephone.

'Mrs Fordyce? Hello, it's Sheila. Yes, very well, thank you. And you? Oh, splendid. I wonder – you know you said I could have that recipe for orange curd? Yes, that's right. Well, I thought I might make some for the coffee morning next month. Would it be an awful nuisance if I popped in for it tomorrow afternoon? After you've had your rest? That's so kind. I'll see you about half past three then. No, I'm afraid I can't stay to tea. Some other time, yes, of course. Goodbye.'

I put down the phone feeling a bit mean. She was a sociable soul and loved visitors. Since my mother's death two years ago (Mother and Peter had died within months of each other – it was a truly dreadful time) she had been rather lonely. There were not very many of her generation left now. But I felt that it would have been very frustrating to have had to sit there imbibing tea and gossip when I wanted to be *doing* something – though I was not sure what exactly I could do, even when I got inside the building.

The following afternoon, with the recipe for orange curd safely in my shopping bag, I got to my feet.

'So sorry I have to dash. And I'd love to come to tea next week. Wednesday would be lovely. No, don't get up. I know my way out by now.'

31

Still chatting, I went to the door and pulled it behind me. Mrs Fordyce's flat was on the ground floor and I didn't want her to see me getting into the lift to go up to the top floor where Lee's flat was.

The lift jerked to a stop and I pulled back the first of the lift gates. Through the bars of the second gate I could see a man standing, waiting to go down. He was short and burly, with a red face and a thick grey moustache. He was dressed in country clothes but somehow he didn't look like a countryman. The olive-green waxed jacket was too clean, the tweed cap too new and the shoes not sturdy enough. He stared at me intently for a moment, and I instinctively clutched my shopping bag to me in a convulsive gesture. The sight of this mundane object seemed to reassure him, and he smiled politely as he drew back the other gate of the lift so that I could get out. I gave a little incoherent murmur as I stepped past him and he closed the lift doors and descended.

This encounter, for some reason, unnerved me slightly, so that I stood for a moment not knowing what to do. Then I moved towards Lee's flat. There was, of course, nothing to be seen, just a closed front door. I had a vague memory of people in films and television plays opening locked doors with plastic credit cards, but, apart from my disinclination to do anything overtly illegal (what would Peter have said?), I wasn't at all sure that I possessed the technical skill. On a sudden impulse I rang the doorbell. There was no reply, and I suppose I would have been surprised and disconcerted if there had been. I was still standing there in something of a daze when the door opposite was opened and an irate voice called out, '*Now* what do you want?'

I turned quickly and saw an elderly lady peering round her door suspiciously. She seemed equally surprised to see me.

'Oh, I thought it was him again.'

'I beg your pardon?'

'That man, who was here just now.'

'Was he looking for Mrs Montgomery too?'

'Yes, he's been several times. Seems very put out to find she's not here.'

'I rather wanted to see Mrs Montgomery myself,' I said, giving her my best WVS smile. 'Is she away?'

The atmosphere lightened a little, and the elderly lady came out on to the landing to converse more easily.

'Yes, I think she must be. I haven't heard her about for quite a while.'

'Oh,' I said brightly, 'what a pity, a wasted journey. I wonder how long she'll be away? Did she cancel her milk?'

She sniffed slightly. 'Oh, she doesn't have anything delivered – no milk, no papers, nothing.' I could tell that she found such behaviour somehow peculiar. 'She keeps herself very much to herself.' I could imagine that Lee would not have bothered to take any trouble with her elderly, unimportant neighbour and would have been totally unconcerned about the impression she made. Unlike me, who always fretted if I wasn't on friendly terms with everyone, however peripheral to my life. I suppose it's a form of cowardice, really.

The elderly woman added, with the air of one who knows her civic duty, 'I did push some letters and circulars through her letter-box a couple of days ago – well, they were sticking out and you never know about burglars and so forth.'

'Oh well.' I smiled again. 'Thank you so much . . . '
I turned and went towards the lift.

When I got to the ground floor I suddenly thought about Lee's garage. They were round at the back of the flats, each one numbered. The door of Lee's was shut, but I put my shopping bag on the ground and crouched down as if to tie up my shoe-lace. There seemed to be no one about, so I peered in through a crack in the pull-down door. It was difficult to see in the dark interior, but eventually I decided that the garage was empty. Wherever Lee was she must, at least to begin with, have been in the green Jaguar.

It was getting dark now, and I moved away before the outside lights of the flats came on. It began to rain, a cold, bitter rain that penetrated my thin headscarf and sent me shivering for the shelter of my car, which I had parked by the harbour wall. I sat there for a while, watching the steel-grey waves hurling themselves monotonously on the shingle, still shivering, as much from a strange kind of numb apprehension as from the cold. Then I switched on the car lights and drove back to my warm, safe house and the comfort of my animals.

Chapter Three

Rosemary's drinks party was well under way when I arrived and she looked a little harassed as she greeted me.

'Oh, Sheila – so glad you've come. Mother's been looking forward to a chat so much.'

She led me over to where her mother was sitting on a sofa by the window. Mrs Dudley was the sort of elderly woman I absolutely loathe. She had been extremely good-looking in her youth, and in old age still seemed to care only for her appearance. She was self-centred, snobbish and difficult and made poor Rosemary's life pretty hellish at times. Today she was wearing an obviously expensive beige and cream knitted suit – cashmere, at a guess. Her make-up was considerably more skilful than mine and her hair was elaborately arranged. She indicated regally that I should join her on the sofa.

'Dear Sheila, so nice to see you.' Her voice was breathy and gushing, too young for her age. She often said effusively how much she admired me for devoting myself to an invalid husband (as if I had ever thought of Peter like that!) and – with a sideways glance at Rosemary – for being such a support to my mother, who had been widowed at an even earlier age than I had been. This always reduced me to a state of incoherent fury, and I longed to say, 'If they had been anything like you, you horrible old bat, I'd have been off like a shot!'

We chatted for some time – or, rather, Mrs Dudley held forth and I murmured sympathetically. She was complaining about These Young People and how casual and slovenly they were in their ways, how unlike *her* day when people *cared* about how they looked and how they behaved. She gesticulated with her hands, and the light caught the diamonds on her plump fingers, the nails painted bright coral pink, but with the tips and half-moons left white in the fashion of the 1930s.

'All this nonsense about Jilly and this young man – a policeman!' She spoke with distaste, and I remembered how Rosemary had never been allowed to make friends with anyone her mother had thought 'unsuitable'. There had been no one more suitable than I – the daughter of a clergyman, whose mother had 'private means' – so that for many years I was Rosemary's only friend.

'And why' – her voice became rather shrill – 'they cannot get married decently like anyone else I cannot imagine. They seem to have no sense of shame ... ' The old-fashioned phrase rattled round my mind and irritated me, so that, although I agreed with her in some ways, I found myself making excuses for them – these uncertain times, economic problems, income tax, even ...

'That's nonsense and you know it,' she declared roundly. 'Right is right and wrong is wrong. *You* would never have done such a thing.'

'I don't know,' I found myself saying, 'nobody ever asked me to.'

She gazed at me in alarm, as if I had suddenly

turned into a stranger, and, indeed, the remark was out of character – or, at least, the character I had always presented to her.

'Sheila!' Jilly was standing behind me and had obviously heard my last remark. She gave me a grateful smile and said, 'Do come and say hello to Roger. I'm longing for you to meet him!'

I slipped back into my role of deferential younger person, telling Mrs Dudley how nice it had been to see her and that I'd have another word before I left, and rapidly followed Jilly across the room.

I could see immediately what had attracted Jilly to Roger in the first place. He was splendidly tall. Jilly, poor girl, was at least five foot ten and had often complained to me that all the really *nice* men were half her size! Roger was well over six foot and decidedly good-looking in a fair, open-air sort of way, which was definitely a bonus. I smiled at him approvingly, for I liked Jilly. She was a cheerful, easy-going girl, who treated me as a contemporary and not a sort of spinster aunt. It is always flattering, as we get older, to find the children of our friends apparently liking us for ourselves and not just as appendages of their parents.

'Roger, this is Sheila. I know you'll both get on. Roger likes books too.'

With this daunting remark she darted away with a plate of canapés.

Roger laughed. 'After that, what can I say?'

'What sort of books?' I asked curiously. 'Sherlock Holmes and Inspector Maigret? What do policemen read?'

'Well, this policeman reads Trollope and George Eliot,' he said. 'And Charlotte M. Yonge. I was very interested in your article on the medical background in *The Daisy Chain*, in the *Review of Literature*.' He smiled at my evident surprise. 'If you think about it, the Victorian novel is the perfect antidote to twentieth-century violence.'

We embarked upon one of those eager conversations that enthusiasts for a comparatively unknown author find so absorbing, interrupting each other to praise our own favourite characters and incidents. We were chatting so easily and so comfortably that I found myself saying, 'Roger, how do the police trace missing people?'

He looked at me sharply and was suddenly a policeman again.

'Why?' he asked. 'Have you lost someone?'

I gave a little laugh. 'Goodness, no,' I said. 'It's just that in plays and novels – I often wonder, when it happens there, why the heroine – it usually is the heroine – never goes to the police, when presumably they could clear the whole thing up, just like that, and do her out of all her adventures!'

He smiled, but his grey eyes were serious. No fool, Jilly's young man.

'Well, actually, apart from the obvious things, like checking hospitals and circulating descriptions, there's not much we can do. Computers make it easier to cover a wide area, of course. But I think you'll find that a very large proportion of people who disappear do so because they want to. They don't want to be found.'

'I suppose so – poor henpecked husbands going off for a bit of peace, bullied wives. Yes, I can see that.'

'There *are* kidnappings, of course, but, honestly, we don't get many of those. And a few people disappear in connection with certain crimes – fraud

38

and so forth. In certain financial situations a strategic withdrawal for a time is sometimes necessary.'

He spoke in a dry, almost academic tone, as though about to embark on a lecture, when we were interrupted again. Mrs Dudley had come up behind us and was about to impose her personality upon this unsuitable young man.

'Now, Roger, I want to hear all about being a policeman.' She made it sound as if he wore size twelve boots and a helmet. 'What made you become one? Was your father in the police force?'

She led him away and Jilly giggled beside me. 'If she thinks she's going to patronise Roger she's got another think coming! He'll give her a very brisk lecture about CID work and then casually let her know that his father was a bishop – I must go and listen!'

On that agreeable note I left the party and drove home in a thoughtful mood. What Roger had said was obviously true. In the light of what Carol had told me, as well as Lee's own remarks about the 'sticky situation' that she needed Charles's help with, it might well have been necessary for her to go away somewhere. But where? And why for so long? And if she needed Charles's help, why hadn't she told him all about it, or at least made some sort of excuse for her absence? She must have known that he would worry if she simply disappeared.

I put the car away and started to make myself a snack lunch – all I needed after the nuts and olives and cheese straws. As I chopped up mushrooms and tomatoes to fry up with some cold mashed potato, my mind was squirrelling round as I tried for the umpteenth time to find some logical explanation of the affair. What did I actually know? Lee had been in the office on Monday 2 January, when she'd had the mysterious phone call that Carol had overheard. She had said she was going away the next day, presumably to meet Jay, whoever *he* was, at Wringcliff Bay, and she hadn't been seen since. It was to be a secret meeting of some sort because she hadn't wanted Carol to know about it. Presumably that phone call was the one she had been expecting ever since she had got back from America. 'Nervy', Carol had said, so it must have been important to her as well as secret. Was it something to do with the dubious business dealings, or was it more personal, something to do with her forthcoming marriage to Charles, a marriage that was, one would have thought, going to solve all her problems?

Wringcliff Bay. Why should she meet anyone there? It was an isolated spot, especially in the depths of winter, so obviously there was some good reason why she didn't want to be seen with Jay.

A peremptory bark brought me back to the present and I went to the back door to let Tris in, and then got on with my lunch. I tried to put the problem to one side, but like those twinges of rheumatism that I get nowadays, it remained with me, just below the level of my consciousness, slight but persistent, all day.

Charles phoned again that evening, though at a more civilised hour than last time.

'Well, Sheila, what have you found out? Where is she? What's happened?'

I hesitated. There was so little to tell, really. Nothing concrete, that is, only an accumulation of little incidents and a general feeling of puzzlement and unease, and that was not what Charles wanted to hear. He liked facts, carefully marshalled and preferably on paper.

'She's not at Country Houses,' I said cautiously, 'and they don't seem to know when she'll be back. And she hasn't been in her flat for quite a while.'

'But *where* is she?'

'My dear Charles,' I replied with some asperity, 'that's what I have spent a great deal of time trying to find out, but I still can't get any sort of lead.'

For some reason, I didn't feel I could tell him about Jay and the phone call, partly because I felt sure he wouldn't know who Jay was anyway, partly to protect Carol, but mostly, quite irrationally, I felt I must protect Lee herself, who obviously didn't want Charles to know anything about it. This was ridiculous, since Charles was an old and dear friend and I didn't even *like* Lee, but there was a sort of instinct, a freemasonry of women, perhaps, that made me keep silent.

'Charles,' I said suddenly, 'was Lee in any sort of financial trouble?'

He hesitated for a moment. 'Well, I suppose I can tell you. There was a sort of cash-flow problem.' Lee's word had been 'static'. 'As a matter of fact, I lent her some money. Not a vast amount, about fifty thousand dollars.'

That certainly seemed a vast amount of money to me, though it *was* dollars rather than pounds, and to someone like Charles who was used to dealing in multi-national millions I suppose it wasn't a lot. Still – I remembered Roger's phrase about 'a strategic withdrawal' sometimes being necessary in fraud cases.

'Well, I suppose it wasn't a loan exactly,' Charles said. 'After all, I'm going to be her partner in the

firm, so I suppose you might call it an investment.'

There was just a hint of defiance in his voice, a
slight defensiveness in case I should think that he
was just another gullible man who had been taken
in by an attractive woman, in spite of his business
acumen and sophisticated life-style. Was this, then,
the simple explanation? I wondered. Just take the
money and run? But that would be very short-
sighted. Charles was a rich man, and there was a
great deal more money where that first instalment
had come from. Lee was no fool, and when we had
talked together she had certainly seemed determined
to marry Charles.

'Oh, well, yes, I do see that,' I said hastily. 'Anyway, I really can't tell you any more. I'll keep my
eyes open and ask around. I'm sorry, Charles, I know
this must be dreadfully worrying and frustrating for
you, being so far away.'

'I wish to God I *could* get over myself,' he said,
'but I have to be in Rio next week to negotiate this
concession – my job depends on it . . . '

I wondered, if I were in Charles's position,
whether I'd have dropped everything and simply
come back to Taviscombe. I expect I would, but
then I am not a man, and a business man at that,
and if Charles lost his job Lee wouldn't want to
marry him anyway.

Charles's voice broke in on my profitless speculations.

'Please do what you can, Sheila. It means an awful
lot to me and you are the only person I can trust to
make enquiries – the others wouldn't understand.
But you have always been so splendid . . . '

I assured Charles that I would continue to do

what I could to find Lee and put the receiver down with the word 'splendid' still echoing in my ears.

What on earth was I doing, I asked myself resentfully, expending all this time and energy on something that, ultimately, didn't concern me? Because I am 'splendid' and can be relied on to do things for other people? Lee meant nothing to me, and although Charles is an old friend and I am fond of him – was more than fond in my early youth – why should I allow this to become almost an obsession?

'Because you are a fool!' I said out loud. Tris, who was sleeping at my feet, raised his head and looked at me in surprise. But I knew, really, the main reason I was trying to help Charles solve his mystery. All my life I have loved 'finding out' about people and speculating about their lives, so that sometimes it seems that I live vicariously other people's lives more intensely than my own. From a very early age I have always invented stories about people I have known only by sight, who have caught my attention in some way. And sometimes I have 'investigated' them – in my youth even shadowing them in the street, like a private detective in fiction – finding out about them obliquely from other sources, looking them up in directories or registers. It began as a sort of game, but over the years it has become part of the fabric of my life, adding a kind of richness. If I were a novelist or an anthropologist I could have called it collecting copy or doing fieldwork, but since I am neither I suppose other people would regard it as an unnatural curiosity. Peter had always been amused at my 'sagas', as we used to call them, and as he gradually became more inactive and housebound he too used to join in my speculations, bringing his legal mind to bear on logical explanations for unusual behaviour in our various subjects. It was a source of harmless amusement to us in those later days of his illness. Since his death I hadn't had the heart to embark on another saga, and Lee's disappearance was, I suppose, a sort of substitute, an extension of our fantasies.

The next day brought no answer to the problem, but I briskly told myself that something would turn up and that in a small town like Taviscombe someone would have noticed something. Mother used to say with a kind of wry resignation that whatever you do in a small seaside town, and even more so in the countryside around, there will always be *someone* watching! This is a fact that people from the towns, crowded and anonymous, never seem to understand.

I enjoy supermarket shopping in the winter. Ours is a vast and cathedral-like store, designed really, I suppose, for the jostling crowds of summer visitors with trolleys crammed with hamburgers, crisps and cans of lager for their self-catering holidays, and their attendant children, alternately grizzling for chocolate or playing noisy games of tag around the frozen-food cabinets. Out of season there is a feeling of space and quiet, so that one can stand motionless in unseeing contemplation of rows of tinned fruit, one's thoughts miles away. It is all very restful.

I had come to rest in just such a fashion when a voice behind me exclaimed, 'Sheila! What luck seeing you here. I was going to ring you.' It was Anthea, unexpectedly sun-tanned and very chatty. 'Ronnie and I have been in Malta for ten days and we're longing to tell *somebody* all about it. We wondered if you'd like to come to dinner next week – Ronnie's cousin from Inverness is staying and I know he'd love to see you again.'

I couldn't help smiling to myself. Now that I was a widow Anthea felt it necessary to provide a spare man when she invited me to dinner, not perhaps with a view to matchmaking, but more from a need to 'make up the numbers' in an old-fashioned way. I remembered Ronnie's cousin from Inverness from other such occasions – a dim little man, interested only in bridge and golf and obviously contemptuous of me when I disclaimed knowledge of either of these pastimes.

'How splendid,' I said insincerely, 'I'd love to come.'

Apparently inspired by this, Anthea pulled a can of lychees from the shelf and put it in her trolley.

'Oh yes,' she said suddenly. 'I knew there was something. Poor old Charles had better look out!'

'What do you mean?' I asked sharply.

'*Well*, that Lee woman. We saw her with another man, miles from anywhere. They seemed very involved, he had his hand on her arm— '

'Where was this and when?'

'Oh, just before we went away, the first week in January – yes that's right, it was the Tuesday. We were on our way to have lunch with my sister – you remember Helen, she lives in Barnstaple, her eldest daughter's a physiotherapist. Tuesdays are the best day for her. Anyway, since it's winter and all those dreadful tourists have gone, we thought we'd go along that little coast road. Well, I mean, you can't do that in the summer – the road's so narrow you have to keep backing all the time, what with

45

all the cars trying to get through to Ilfracombe. As Ronnie says, there really ought to be a signpost saying that it's not a through road. It's downright dangerous with that sheer drop to the sea on one side, and most of the visitors haven't the least idea of backing a car – well, I suppose they never have to in the town – they try to squeeze past in the most impossible places. Honestly, it makes my blood run cold, and Ronnie's language— '

'But what about Lee?'

'Lee? Oh yes, well, as I was saying, we were driving along that coast road and you know the bit just beyond the Valley of Rocks, it's all wooded and there's an open bit where you can get on to the cliffs – it's a glorious view, with the sea miles below and all those rocks and that little bay, what's it called? Anyway, that Jaguar of hers was parked in the passing place there, and a Land Rover, and there was Lee and this man walking along the cliff-top, and just as we passed he put his hand on her arm, like I said. I wanted to stop but Ronnie wouldn't – men are so stuffy about that sort of thing – so I couldn't see any more,' she finished regretfully.

'How did she look?' I asked.

'Look? Well, I don't know the woman all that well. Actually though, now I come to think of it, she did look a bit agitated. Well, she would, wouldn't she? I mean, carrying on like that when she's supposed to be practically engaged to Charles, and a car coming by – you wouldn't expect any traffic along that road at this time of the year. Not that she could have seen who was in it, but for all she knew it *might* have been someone who would tell Charles what she was up to, and then where would all her scheming to catch him get her!'

'How do you mean, agitated?'

'Well, she shook off his arm quite violently. But then, if you lead a man on you should know what to expect. *She's* no innocent girl!'

Anthea's voice took on a shrill note and I found myself perversely disliking her for her dislike of Lee.

I felt I needed time and solitude to take in what Anthea had told me, so I simply said, 'Goodness, how *extraordinary*!' and turned my shopping trolley as if to move away.

'You're more in touch with Charles than the rest of us,' Anthea said. 'I do think you ought to tell him about it. I told Ronnie someone should but he said it was none of our business, but *I* think Charles should know what's going on behind his back.'

I made some noncommittal sound.

'Anyway,' Anthea reverted to her original theme, 'do come to dinner. Next Friday, about seven for seven thirty.'

'Thank you, I'll look forward to it.'

Thankfully, I moved across to the checkout, although I had by no means finished my shopping, but I had to get away from Anthea's chatter and try to sort things out in my own mind.

I walked down the Avenue, past the shops that in the summer sold gifts and cheap clothing, now shuttered and empty. A few of the windows had lettering scrawled across them: 'GREAT CLOSING DOWN SALE', 'FINAL REDUCTIONS'. There was something sad, even pathetic, about them, on a grey afternoon when the light was beginning to fade and the world seemed at a very low ebb. I was overcome by a feeling of melancholy, a sort of dragging down of the spirits, and I walked slowly towards the sea-wall. In times of sadness or stress, or even of bewilderment, I always go down and look at the sea. I rested my shopping bag on the wall and looked at the waves creaming across the sand and breaking on the shingle and at the sea-birds dipping and delving at the water's edge. The lights were coming on on the far side of Taviscombe Bay, and across the Bristol Channel there were smudges of light that were Port Talbot and Margam in Wales.

So Jay *was* a man and Lee had met him as she had arranged. But what sort of meeting had it been? Anthea's description of Lee violently shaking off his arm made me wonder if there had been some sort of struggle. I remembered that stretch of coast very well. We used to go to Wringcliff Bay for picnics when I was a child and my father was still alive. It was a beautiful little bay, quite secluded, and summer visitors never seemed to find it. I suppose the path down was too steep and overhung with brambles and wild clematis for them to take the trouble.

One summer, when I was about seven, we had made our way happily down to the beach and I was wandering along the shore looking for shells while my parents were unpacking the picnic basket. I rounded a rock and suddenly came upon the body of a goat. The wild goats who lived along that part of the coast were famous, and I loved to watch them delicately picking their way along the rocky cliff-face. It appeared from the stones lying around the body that part of the cliff had given way, and the goat had fallen on to the rocks below. I had never seen death before but I knew immediately that the creature was dead. In the one look that I had taken before I turned, shuddering, away, I had seen that its creamy fawn coat was matted with blood and that the scavenging birds had already begun their work.

I went back to my parents but I didn't tell them what I had seen. Somehow it seemed too private and personal a grief to share with anyone. I ate very little of our picnic tea, and as we climbed up the cliff-path I looked down and was just able to make out the pathetic little body lying on the sand. Looking across Taviscombe sands with the gulls crying, as they had done on that day long ago, the picture came back to me, but this time it was Lee's body that I saw, with the birds wheeling above it.

Chapter Four

I awoke early next morning, and somehow it seemed best to get up and do prosaic jobs about the house to distract my mind from a growing sense of unease. I deliberately chose my least favourite tasks – scrubbing out the kitchen bin and putting in a new plastic bag, scraping the burnt bits from underneath the grill in the cooker, and, finally, in a burst of energy, cleaning the stairs with that infuriating vacuum attachment that winds itself round your legs like an insidious python. But all the time I was working I couldn't get out of my head the picture of Lee struggling with a man on the edge of the path leading down to Wringcliff Bay.

I switched off the vacuum, and Tris and Foss, who both hate it, materialised and demanded food. As I was opening tins, I made a sudden decision. I would rid my mind of all my silly fancies by driving over to Wringcliff Bay and assuring myself that of course there was no body lying on the beach. It was a nice bright morning, and not as cold as it had been for the last few weeks, so it would be a pleasant little outing.

As I drove along the lanes I saw a figure on a horse, and as I approached I realised that it was Marjorie Fraser. She always looked unexpectedly elegant in her neatly tied stock, navy jacket, cream breeches and beautiful leather boots. From the formality of her attire I gathered that she was going hunting – she had been complaining the other day that the ground had been too hard to get out since the New Year. I slowed down and drove very slowly and cautiously round her, since her horse was backing and sidling in what one writer has called 'the divinely silly way' of horses. I waved as I passed, and she touched the peak of her cap with her riding crop and smiled at me. She really was quite a different person when she was on a horse, relaxed, cheerful and friendly, and I pondered, not for the first time, on the strange complexity of all human beings.

As I came up to the top of Porlock Hill I saw that the hunt was already assembling. Since I was born and brought up in hunting country I know all the arguments, for and against, but, being a fool about animals, I must say that I can't bear to think of any animal being hunted, for whatever reason. And yet . . . Whenever I actually see the hunt, as I did that morning, I can't resist stopping to have a look and to admire the picture they make – the beauty of the horses, the elegance of the riders and the fascination of the questing hounds. And if I catch a glimpse of them in full flight, strung out across the bracken-covered hillside, then I get an irrational thrill and a sort of aesthetic pleasure.

As I drove along the main coast road towards Lynton I came to the turning Lee had taken on that last morning I had seen her, the turning to Plover's Barrow. On an impulse, I turned left along it and made my way through the narrow lanes until I came to the entrance to the drive. Feeling rather foolish, and wondering what I would do if anyone appeared and challenged my right to be there, I drove on towards the house. I caught a glimpse of the chimneys through the bare branches of the trees, and then something that made me catch my breath sharply. Parked in front of the house was Lee's green Jaguar.

I drove up behind it and sat for a moment, wondering what to do. I didn't, somehow, feel capable of consecutive thought, and acted simply on instinct. I got out of the car, went over to the front door and rang the bell. I stood for several minutes and then rang again, but there was no reply. So I went round the side of the house, as I had done with Lee, past the stables, and knocked on the kitchen door. Again there was silence. As I stood there, irresolute, there was a strange snuffling, scuffling sound and I swung round quickly. Just beyond the back hedge was the open moor, and a group of wild ponies, made bold by the winter cold, had gathered by the back gate and were pressing near, hoping that someone was bringing them hay or other food, as people did in the really hard weather.

This little incident made me pull myself together and think what I should do. Boldly, I tried the back door, but it was locked, so I moved along and looked through the large, uncurtained kitchen window. For a moment I didn't take in the reality of what I saw. Lying on the floor was a woman, face down, with a large kitchen knife sticking out of her back. As I had done with the body of the goat all those years ago, I looked quickly away, but I was no longer seven years old: I was not a child, I had to look again, to take in the full, unspeakable details of what I had seen so fleetingly.

I forced myself to look through the window. It

was Lee, as I had known in my heart that it would be. She was lying stretched out on the floor, her face hidden, but the ash blonde hair was unmistakable, and on her outflung arm was the heavy gold charm bracelet that Rosemary and I had commented on rather cattily after the first time we had met her. The straight skirt of her dark grey suit had hitched up as she fell, and one high-heeled shoe had fallen off and lay on its side beside her. I forced myself to look at the knife that had been driven into her back. It was an old-fashioned, bone-handled carving knife, of the kind that people used to use for poultry – I have one myself, that belonged to my grandmother.

I felt deathly cold and found that I was shivering uncontrollably. I couldn't move, my legs simply wouldn't work. 'Oh God,' I found myself whispering, 'Oh God.' I clenched my hands, driving the nails into my palms, to bring some life, some sort of feeling, back into my body. I must have stood there for several minutes – it felt like hours; time was suspended, as, I felt, were all natural laws. Eventually my brain accepted the evidence of my eyes and told me that Lee had been murdered.

I should, I suppose, have got into the house somehow, broken a window, or something, to make sure that Lee was indeed dead and that there was nothing I could do to help her, but I am ashamed to say that I couldn't bring myself even to look through the window again. A violent sense of physical revulsion gripped me, and I turned away. I went back and sat in my car. It didn't occur to me that Lee's murderer might still be around – I knew, even from that relatively brief inspection, that her body had been lying there for some time, alone in that cold dank

53

house. I drew in a harsh, shuddering breath at the thought.

I switched on the car engine and turned the heater fan full on and, gradually, as the merciful warmth brought me back to life again, I tried to pull myself together. I remembered that there was a telephone box on the main coast road just before the turning off to Plover's Barrow. I turned the car clumsily, almost scraping the side of the Jaguar as I did so, and drove back the way I had come. The phone box was silhouetted against the sky at the top of a steep incline. It looked like the last phone box in the world.

I got through to the Taviscombe police and was surprised to hear my own voice explaining clearly, carefully and unemotionally what had happened, giving them my name and describing the exact location of Plover's Barrow, while all the time my senses were in turmoil and I honestly didn't really know where I was or what I was doing. The police sergeant asked me to go back to the house and wait for them – he hoped they wouldn't be more than half an hour – if I didn't mind. I agreed mechanically and rang off.

Now that I had actually done something, made an effort, I felt calmer as I got back into the car. I drove very slowly back to the house, spinning out the time so that I wouldn't have so long to wait there alone. I parked in the drive, a little way back from the Jaguar, and waited. After a while I put on the radio, but it was one of those consumer affairs programmes and I felt that the problem of non-functioning washing machines was trivial and irrelevant in the present situation. It was cold sitting there, and I got out of the car to walk about a bit to get my circulation going. I approached the Jaguar and tried the door handle. It was locked – Lee was obviously taking no chances with her precious car, even out here. I looked through the window. On the back seat there was a briefcase, half open, with what looked like property descriptions spilling out of it. There was also a cream leather dressing case and the fawn suede jacket that Lee had been wearing the first time I had seen her.

I turned away to go back to my own car, but my hands were cold, even with my gloves on, and my car keys slipped through my fingers. As I bent down to pick them up, I noticed the tyre tracks – there was only one set. As I mentioned before, we had had quite a lot of frost in these first weeks of January. On New Year's Day it had poured with rain the whole day – I remember that everyone said what a dismal start to the New Year it was – and the following couple of days had been unseasonably mild. But after that, there had been a continuous heavy frost, until now, really. The ground was still too hard for my tyres to have made any impression, so Lee must have come here on the 3rd or the 4th. And she must have come alone, or brought her murderer with her. Suddenly I fully realised that Lee was not just dead, but that she had been murdered. Someone had actually killed her, had driven that kitchen knife into her body, through the resisting flesh. Someone had hated her that much. All my new-found calm disappeared, and I was shaking again, frightened now as well as distressed. I got back into my car and locked all the doors – a futile gesture, I suppose – and sat there with my eyes shut and my hands tightly clasped together, hunched over the steering wheel, waiting for the police to arrive.

I heard several cars driving up and opened my eyes. There was a white police car and a dark red Sierra. The door of this opened and two men in plain clothes got out. One of them was Roger. I wrenched open the door of my car and ran towards him, calling his name. He caught me by the arm and led me gently to his car and sat me down in the passenger seat.

'It's all right, Sheila,' he said, 'we're here now. It's a horrible thing to have happened.'

I said incoherently, 'I didn't go in – I couldn't. I should have seen if I could do anything, but— '

'You did absolutely the right thing. Much better to leave things exactly as they were.'

'But she might have been alive. I feel so dreadful about it . . . ' My voice was rising and I was sobbing. He said soothingly, 'It's all right, hang on.'

He leaned over and reached into the back of the car. 'Here we are then, I'm sure Sergeant Coleford won't mind if we borrow some of his coffee.' He unscrewed the cup of the vacuum flask and poured some out. 'Now then, try some of this.' The coffee was very milky, and so hot that it burned the roof of my mouth, but I drank it gratefully and felt the wave of hysteria that had threatened me receding.

'Oh, thank you, that's better – I'm sorry I was so stupid.'

'Not stupid at all – perfectly natural. Now, you stay here and have a spot more coffee and I'll come back as soon as I can.'

He got out of the car and joined the others and they went round the back of the house.

I sat there quite calmly. I felt better now, as much from the sudden burst of sobbing as from the hot coffee. Catharsis, I thought, and then despised myself for having such a literary thought on such an occasion. I allowed my mind to go blank, and sat there, my hands clasped round the warm cup, staring at the activity before me.

After a while Roger returned.

'Feel better now?' he asked.

'Yes, indeed I do,' I replied. 'Thank you so much.'

He got back into the car, and I suddenly realised something.

'Roger, why are *you* here? I mean, it's marvellous that it should be you, but why?'

'Pure coincidence. I was at the Taviscombe station when your call came through, and when I heard your name and that you had found the body, I asked Inspector Dean if I could come along. I knew what a shock it must have been. People don't realise – finding someone like that – it's very traumatic.'

'I'm very grateful. It was such a shock – though I suppose I might have guessed . . . '

Roger looked at me keenly. 'Was she the one who had disappeared?'

I nodded.

'I thought so,' he said. 'You can always tell – you suddenly became very vague! I think you had better tell me all about it, don't you?'

So I told him about Charles's phone call and how strange it had seemed, and how no one had seen Lee since the beginning of January. I didn't tell him about Jay though, or about the shady business dealings, because I thought I must let Carol tell him about that herself.

'There really was so little to go on,' I said, not quite honestly.

'Well, there seems to have been enough for you to have come here. Why did you do that?'

I gave a nervous laugh. 'A sort of instinct, I suppose. I know it sounds silly. But, well, I was driving in this direction and I remembered the turning. I came here with Lee just before Christmas to pick up the keys from the caretaker – she was hoping to do a good deal on the property.'

As I spoke I felt that my explanation sounded rather thin, but Roger appeared to accept it as perfectly reasonable.

'Had she any relations?'

'I don't think so. I suppose there is a *Mr* Montgomery – she's divorced, I believe. I just know what Charles told me – I only met her a couple of times.'

'Yes, of course. Well, Inspector Dean will be dealing with all that.'

'Yes. Roger – I imagine you've noticed – but you see there's only one set of tyre marks ... '

He smiled. 'Very Sherlock Holmes. Yes, I had noticed. Until the pathology people have had a go and we've established exactly when she died, we can't get a proper picture.'

I felt slightly dishonest, not giving him all the information I had, but the police would find it all out soon enough – I could leave it to them now.

Roger was looking at me earnestly. 'Now, are you going to be all right to drive yourself? I could take you back and get someone else to collect your car ... '

'Oh, goodness, no. I'm perfectly all right now. It was just the shock – you know.'

He looked slightly relieved, and I realised that

although he was not officially involved in the case he wanted to look around for himself.

'Inspector Dean will want a statement, of course, this afternoon or tomorrow.'

'Yes, of course. I'll have pulled myself together by then and should be a bit more coherent! I suppose I'll have to telephone Charles – I'm *not* looking forward to that! Is it all right if I tell Rosemary?'

'Yes, certainly. I suppose she might know a bit more about Lee Montgomery.'

'I shouldn't think so – I don't think she knew her any more than I did.' I had a sudden thought. 'I tell you what, though, I bet old Mrs Dudley – you know, Jilly's grandmother – knows something. She knows absolutely everything about everybody in Taviscombe – preferably something to their discredit!'

Roger grinned. 'I can well believe it!' he said. 'Right, then, off you go. Have a good stiff drink when you get back and a long chat with Rosemary – very therapeutic – shake off the horrors!'

He saw me into my car and waved cheerfully as I drove off. As I went along the drive I looked in my rear mirror and saw him heading purposefully for the house. It wouldn't surprise me, I thought, if he somehow got himself attached to this investigation. I hoped he would, because I had a high opinion of his competence and I wanted this horrible mess to be sorted out as soon as possible.

The bright winter sun had vanished, and as I drove back swirls of mist and low cloud hid the moor on either side of the road. It was dank and clammy and deeply depressing. Even with the car heater on I felt cold, right down into my bones. Somehow I didn't feel ready to go back home. I wasn't ready yet to explain what had happened or face Rosemary's excited questioning.

I drove into the deserted picnic area at the top of Porlock Common and turned off the engine. Everything was quiet and still. The silence felt almost as tangible as the mist around me. The trees and brown grass were sodden with moisture, everything looked totally dead. Not far away I heard a faint sound. It was the thin note of a horn. The huntsman was blowing 'Gone Away'.

I was just considering the dreadful irony of this when I heard a crashing and clattering around me and several horsemen trotted by. I was aware of someone on a horse stopping near my car. I wound down the window and saw to my dismay that it was Marjorie Fraser. She dismounted and led her horse towards me. It was uncertain of the car and kept shying away.

'Are you all right?' she asked. 'I thought that was your car and I wondered if you'd broken down or something.'

My first, totally unworthy thought was that I wished she would mind her own business and leave me alone. The last thing I wanted at this moment was Marjorie Fraser being helpful and organising.

'No, I'm quite all right, it's not that.' I had no intention of telling her what had happened, but I found myself blurting out, 'The fact is – I've just found Lee Montgomery's body – she's been murdered!'

Marjorie's horse suddenly plunged and reared and she had to give all her attention to holding him. When he was quiet she tied him to a fence and came over to me. She put her face in through the open window of the car and looked incredulously at me.

'*What* did you say you had found?'

'Lee Montgomery – do you know her? She was going to marry our friend, Charles Richardson . . . '

'Yes, I've met her a couple of times.' Marjorie's face was grim, the corners of her mouth turned down – I couldn't imagine that she and Lee would have been much in sympathy with each other. 'Her *body* did you say?'

She seemed to imply that I was having some sort of delusion.

'Yes, at a place called Plover's Barrow – up and over the hill. She'd been stabbed.'

'What on earth were you doing *there*?' There was a familiar hectoring note in her voice – the sort of voice that made your hackles rise, Rosemary said – that she used when she was 'determined to get to the bottom of all this' at committee meetings.

I had just decided resentfully (a state of mind she usually reduced me to) that I really wasn't going to allow myself to be cross-examined by Marjorie Fraser, when another rider called out to her and she went over to speak to him. When she came back I had switched on the engine and simply said, 'I have to get back now – I'll tell you all about it later,' and made my escape.

The irritability that that little encounter induced did me good, and I felt much more normal as I drove home. I went into the house, and it seemed incredible that everything should be just as I had left it that morning. Tris rushed to greet me, leaping up as high as his short legs would let him. Foss strolled negligently downstairs, yawning after a long sleep all morning under the duvet on my bed. I patted Tris and rolled him over on to his back, and he barked delightedly. I snatched Foss up to me and held him against my face. He purred loudly and then, impatient, struggled and wailed to be put down.

'Come on, you two,' I said. 'Let's open a tin.'

Chapter Five

I had a call from the police station early the following morning asking me to go and make a statement
at twelve o'clock. It was my day for the hospital
run and I had to take old Mrs Aston in for her
physiotherapy at ten o'clock, so I had plenty of
time. As I helped her out of the car and balanced
her on her walking frame, she said, in her usual
plaintive way, 'Will you be able to stay and take
me back? You never know how long it's going to
be. They *say* half an hour, but it could be any time
and it's ever so cold in that passage . . . '

Swallowing my irritation, I assured Mrs Aston
that of *course* I would call and take her back home,
as I always did, and she tottered off into the Out
Patients department.

The back of the hospital was almost opposite
Country Houses, and as I looked across the road
I saw a police car driving away. A light was on so
I thought I would just pop in and see how Carol
had got on with the police. She looked startled
and frightened as the door opened, but when she
saw that it was me a look of relief flooded over
her face.

'Oh, Mrs Malory, I'm so glad to see you. I was
going to ring you!'

'They've told you the dreadful news then, Carol? About poor Mrs Montgomery?'

'I really can't believe it – well, you never think, do you, that something like that can happen to someone you know! And to think that she was lying there like that all this time . . . it's really awful.' She looked at me in great distress. 'It must have been terrible for you, finding her like that. When they told me it was you I thought, poor Mrs Malory, what a terrible thing, finding someone like that!' She seemed more upset at the idea of my finding the body than that Lee was dead.

'It was a terrible shock,' I said, 'but the police were very kind and helpful. I suppose they wanted to know when Mrs Montgomery was last in the office.'

Carol fidgeted with some papers. 'Yes, well, I didn't tell them much – just that she hadn't been in since January the second. And they looked at the appointment book and saw the entry for January the fourth. That's all really.'

'But didn't you tell them about the phone conversation, about Jay?'

She looked defiant. 'I'm not going to get mixed up in all this,' she said. 'You know what the police are like.'

'Oh Carol, really, you *must* give them all the help you can. You want them to find out who did this terrible thing, don't you? And what about those property dealings that you thought were a bit dodgy – you must tell them about that.'

'No fear! They'd only think I had something to do with it, and if *she's* not here any more they'll want someone to blame. They'll fit you up as soon as look at you, that's what Derek always said!'

I tried to reason with her, but it is difficult to persuade a person who has lived with someone on the wrong side of the law, as she had done when she was married to Derek, to trust the police.

'Honestly, Mrs Malory, I just can't.' She looked round nervously, though we were obviously quite alone. 'Look, I'll tell *you* – but you must promise not to let them know I told you.'

I felt very uneasy about this compromise and wished passionately that Peter was here to advise me. But Carol was adamant and I supposed this was better than nothing.

'Well, all right then, Carol. Tell me what you know.'

'It was that Mr Bradford—'

'*Councillor* Bradford?'

'Yes, that's him. I heard bits of phone conversations and heard them talking sometimes. She didn't know I was listening half the time, or when she did she probably thought I was too stupid to put two and two together.' Carol had certainly disliked Lee, I thought. And Lee had seriously under-rated Carol.

'What was it all about?'

'I'm not really sure, but it seemed to me that Mrs Montgomery was buying property for him, but not in his own name. That's illegal, isn't it?'

'It certainly is. Whereabouts was this property?'

'All in the same area – just outside Taunton. There was an old garage that had been closed down for quite a bit – very run-down – and some cottages and a small farm and a bit of land. I don't know if that was all. As I say, I had to piece it all together. And, he never came here – not after the first time. She sent me out then, to get some stationery – just to get me out of the office. Anyway, like I say, he never came to the office again. He rang sometimes and I think he went to her flat.'

I had a sudden thought. 'Is he a shortish man with a red face and a grey moustache?'

'Yes, that's right. Do you know him?'

'I think,' I said evasively, 'that I must have seen his picture in the *Echo*.' And, indeed, now I came to think of it, I remembered smudgy newsprint photos of a man, very like the one I had seen coming away from Lee's flat that day. 'Councillor Bradford, Councillor Philip Bradford – P.B.! Do you think *he* was the person she was meeting on the fourth?'

Carol seemed less excited than I was at this piece of deduction.

'I shouldn't think she'd have put it in her appointments book if it was him – she never put anything on paper about all that – not in the office. There's nothing here now, anyway. I went through all the papers while she was away.' She looked slightly shamefaced. 'Well, I had to protect myself. If there had been anything – well, I couldn't afford to get mixed up in it – not with the children and all. *You* understand that, Mrs Malory.'

I thought of how relatively lucky I had been, of the kindness and loving support I had had when Peter died, and there had always been enough money for Michael and for me. Who was I to judge Carol?

'Yes, of course I understand,' I said gently. 'Which reminds me. Mr Fordyce, the dentist, you know, at the end of the Avenue, is looking for a new receptionist. I saw his wife the other day and she said that Molly, who's with him now, is leaving – her husband's moving to Yeovil, I think. It might be worth while giving him a ring and asking. You can give me as a reference if you like.'

I felt a slight qualm at the thought of giving a reference to someone who was withholding information from the police, but I told myself stoutly that Mr Fordyce was hardly likely to put Carol in the same position that Lee had done! And after all, in the long run, Carol was doing what she was doing for the sake of her children. Surely no one would blame her for that.

Carol's enthusiastic burst of gratitude embarrassed me, and I drew on my gloves and got up to go.

'And you won't let the police know anything I told you – about the phone call and the property deals?'

'Not for now – I expect they'll find out about them from someone else, anyway,' I said with an air of false assurance.

I collected Mrs Aston, who was complaining that there was no coffee machine in the waiting area like there was 'up Taunton', and drove her back to her cottage. There was just half an hour before I had to go to the police station so I went into the Buttery for a cup of coffee and tried to decide exactly what I was going to tell them.

I was glad to see that there was no one I knew in the Buttery, but I took my coffee (having regretfully resisted a Danish pastry) into the far corner away from the window and sat with my back to the door, just to be on the safe side. I badly needed to get my mind clear before I saw the police. Since Carol hadn't told them about the phone call or about Councillor Bradford, then neither would I. My conscience was definitely uneasy at withholding information, but to tell them about it now

67

would only get Carol into trouble. Still, they'd be getting into Lee's flat and perhaps there they would find papers about the property deals and even some reference to the mysterious Jay. And there seemed no point in my telling them something as vague as Anthea's sighting of Lee and that man by the cliff-path. Anyway, if I knew Anthea she'd be off hot-foot down to the police station with *that* little tit-bit as soon as she heard the news – she couldn't resist! All I needed to do, then, was to tell them about Charles and his anxiety and about my meeting with Lee before Christmas and our visit to Plover's Barrow. Put like that it seemed fairly straightforward. If they thought my reason for going back to Plover's Barrow yesterday was a bit peculiar, then I hoped that they would just put me down as a slightly neurotic, middle-aged female and not question it too much.

Inspector Dean was a small, wiry man with thinning dark hair. His manner was brisk and cheerful and he greeted me as an old acquaintance.

'Mrs Malory, how nice to see you again. Mrs Dean and I had the pleasure of meeting you and your husband a few years ago at a Law Society Dinner. I was so sorry to hear about your husband – it must have been a very trying time for you.'

I had a vague memory of the occasion and of meeting a jolly little woman in royal blue crêpe, and I triumphantly salvaged a piece of information from my memory.

'Your daughter was just going up to Oxford, wasn't she, to read Chemistry at *my* old college. How is she doing?'

He looked pleased and said, 'Oh, very well. She got a very good result in her finals and they want her to stay on and do research. Her mother and I are very pleased, as you can imagine.'

'Isn't that marvellous. You must be so proud. Doesn't time fly! My son is up at Oxford now – I was so glad that Peter knew he'd got a place before he died.'

The Inspector pulled out a chair for me and offered me a cup of coffee.

'No thank you, I had one just before I came.'

'Right, then, I suppose we'd better get a statement from you about this nasty business.'

He called in a constable, who sat at the end of the table prepared to write. I told him as succinctly as I could about the phone call from Charles and how I had offered to make enquiries for him and had drawn a blank, and how, after the second call, I had suddenly thought about Plover's Barrow. 'A sort of *hunch*, really' – I used the word deliberately, as being suitable for an investigation. I didn't feel I could get away with 'a woman's intuition', yet, in a way, that's what it was that had made me turn left along the road to Plover's Barrow when what I had in my mind was Wringcliff Bay.

He questioned me closely about my encounter with Lee and our visit to the house before Christmas and I repeated, word for word, what I could remember of our conversation.

'So you think that Mrs Montgomery had definitely decided to marry Mr Richardson, then?'

'Oh yes – well, she seemed determined to let me know that.'

'And she thought that you might be hostile?'

'Not *hostile*. Just a bit anxious for Charles's happiness, if you know what I mean. I've known him since we were children, and all his friends – well –

we wondered if she was the right person to make him happy. But it was his life, after all . . . '

'Yes, I see. But you didn't really like her?'

'I hardly knew her – I suppose she just wasn't my sort of person, if you know what I mean.'

'Yes, I see. Well now, we've had a preliminary pathology report, and as far as they can judge she was killed around January the fourth – the house was cold so the body didn't deteriorate as it would have done in the summer.'

'I shouldn't think that house would ever be really warm,' I said irrelevantly. 'I did feel bad that I didn't try to get in and see if she really was dead – but, honestly, it was such a dreadful shock . . . '

'Just as well you didn't, Mrs Malory. It was best that nothing was disturbed.'

'Did you find any clues? Can you tell me anything?'

'No fingerprints on the knife, if that's what you mean – but then everybody knows about wearing gloves nowadays – all that detective fiction.' He gave me a brief smile. 'But it's early days yet and we're still feeling our way.'

'Yes, of course.'

'Now then, Mrs Malory, perhaps you could give me some idea of what *you* were doing on January the fourth.'

I had become so used to the idea of myself as a detective that to be considered as a suspect startled me considerably. My astonishment must have been very apparent because Inspector Dean said soothingly, 'We're just clearing the ground.'

I gave a slight laugh. 'Of course. And I *did* discover the body, didn't I. In a detective story that would make me a prime suspect!'

I fished in my handbag and found my diary.

'Hang on – January the fourth. Michael was still on holiday, so we went into Taunton to the sales to try and get him some respectable underwear. I do believe he cleans his bike with some of his shirts! Yes, and then after that, on our way back from Taunton, I dragged him to tea with my old aunt who lives at Bishops Lydeard. We didn't leave there till well after six. Just under an hour to get back – yes, I remember, I was rather cross because I'd missed my favourite soap opera! And we spent the rest of the evening quietly at home.'

'Thank you, Mrs Malory. That's fine. I'll just get the Constable here to type it out for you to sign. If there's anything else, we'll be in touch.'

'Inspector – just one thing . . . Did she die straight away – I mean, did she lie there suffering? I shall have to tell Charles, and it would be so much kinder if . . . '

'It would seem that death was more or less instantaneous. Whoever did it knew just where to put the knife, or if he didn't then it was a lucky guess – well, lucky for him!'

'You say "him"?'

'Well, a manner of speaking, really. Though the blow seems to have been struck from above, by someone taller than she was, and she was of medium height.'

'I see. Tell me – will Roger – Inspector Norton be involved in the investigation?'

'We will be reporting back to Taunton CID, certainly, and we use their computer facilities and so forth. Yes, I expect he'll be in touch about it.'

'I just asked – he was so kind and sympathetic

yesterday. He is sort of a friend of a friend,' I said confusedly.

Inspector Dean chose to ignore this explanation – as well he might – and simply said, 'It must have been a very nasty experience for you, especially as you knew the lady.'

'I suppose I feel rather awful because I didn't really care for her as a person – I'm only really sad because of poor Charles.' A thought struck me. 'Will you be in touch with him in Cincinnati? I mean, I was going to ring him tonight – I couldn't bring myself to do it last night, I'm afraid – will that be all right?'

'Yes, indeed – you go ahead and we will be in touch when we know just what we want to ask him about all this.'

The Constable returned with my statement and I signed it, feeling slightly as if I were committing perjury. I wondered again what Peter would say – a legal document was very sacred to him.

Inspector Dean held out his hand. 'Goodbye Mrs Malory. Thank you very much,' he said in a friendly but non-committal way.

As the glass doors swung to behind me, I stood on the top step and drew in a deep breath of fresh air, not only to dispel the warm stuffy air of the police station, but also to savour an almost irresponsible feeling of freedom. I got into my car and drove sedately away.

As I got into the house the phone was ringing. It was Rosemary. I had told her briefly the night before what had happened and she had been loving and sympathetic. But I hadn't wanted to go over and over the ground with her and had pleaded tiredness and rung off quickly. I prepared to fend off her questions again, but it was she who wanted to be brief.

'Isn't it sickening?' she said. 'I was longing to have a real chat with you about it all, but I've got this *miserable* virus thing that's going round and I feel absolutely *awful*. And the thing is, I promised to drive Mother to the chiropodist this afternoon. *Could* you be an angel? I know she could get a taxi, but you know how mean she is about things like that. Besides, it's getting difficult to find a taxi-driver in Taviscombe she hasn't quarrelled with. I'm awfully sorry to have to ask you at such short notice . . . '

I assured Rosemary that I didn't mind in the least and arranged to pick up Mrs Dudley at three o'clock.

'Take care of yourself,' I said, 'and go straight back to bed – Jack can perfectly well make his own supper when he comes in!'

'Well, he'll have to,' Rosemary said. 'The thought of food is absolutely *unendurable*.'

'Is there anything I can get you in the way of shopping while I'm in the town?' I asked.

'There probably is something, but I'm not really capable of rational thought at the moment . . . Oh dear, sorry, I have to dash again!' She rang off abruptly.

I ate a quick sandwich and changed into a suit more worthy of Mrs Dudley. I drove her to the chiropodist and hung about for half an hour and then collected her and drove her back to her large house on the outskirts of Taviscombe. She was very full of the praises of the chiropodist. He was a new man in the practice, and according to Mrs Dudley a vast improvement on the others. I wondered how long this enthusiasm would last – it was unlikely to be long. Soon, like all the other 'marvellous little men' she had discovered, he would be 'absolutely useless' and she would be looking around for someone new.

'Now then,' she said, 'you must come in and have a cup of tea.'

I protested that I had other things I must do, but she waved them aside and I found myself in the familiar drawing room where Rosemary and I had had so many tea-times together, desperately trying not to catch each other's eye so that we wouldn't giggle.

A round table was laid with a lace-edged cloth and I noticed that I was now deemed worthy of the best Royal Worcester china.

'Oh good, Elsie's got everything ready.' Elsie was the down-trodden little woman who had been Mrs Dudley's slave ever since I could remember. She must have been well on into her seventies, but still looked much as she did when Rosemary and I were children. She came in now with the silver tea-pot and hot-water jug and exclaimed with pleasure at seeing me again. I asked after her little dog, and her face lit up as she embarked on a rambling story about how he had learnt to open the kitchen door himself. ('Would you believe *that* Mrs Malory!') Mrs Dudley cut her short. 'We're ready for the tea-cakes now, Elsie.' And Elsie scuttled away to return in a few minutes with hot buttered tea-cakes on the green dish with the raised design of cherries round the edge that I always used to covet.

Having tea with Mrs Dudley was like slipping back in time to another world, which would have been delightful if only one didn't have to listen to her conversation, which was largely malicious gossip about practically everybody in the town. I tried to concentrate on the excellent food (two sorts of jam and three kinds of home-made cake as well as the tea-cakes – at this rate I wouldn't need any supper). But suddenly she had my full attention.

'Rosemary told me about that Montgomery woman being murdered – she says that *you* found her. I could hardly believe it. Rubbish, I told her, a nice girl like Sheila wouldn't go getting herself mixed up in a dreadful thing like that!'

'Not mixed up exactly, Mrs Dudley,' I said. I tried to explain as factually and unsensationally as possible what had happened, and fortunately I mentioned Charles's name and she was immediately diverted.

'Well, *he's* well out of it. And I'd tell him so to his face. She was obviously only after his money. A very hard sort of woman – you know what these so-called "business women" are.'

'Did you know her at all?' I asked.

'I made it my business to go and have a look at her when she first set up that estate agent place. I went in and asked about details of houses – said I was considering something smaller, though of course I wouldn't dream of living anywhere but here. We came here when we were first married, you know . . . Where was I? Oh yes, that Montgomery woman. Very smarmy – sly I would call it. Wouldn't trust her an inch. Just what I expected. Which is what I told Mrs Hertford.'

'Mrs Hertford?' I was now completely confused.

'Well, yes, of *course*.' The breathy voice sank to a whisper and she leaned forward confidentially. 'The Montgomery woman was her daughter-in-law, you know.'

Chapter Six

For a moment I couldn't take in what she was saying.

'Her – what!'

'Her daughter-in-law. She's the one who went off with Jamie Hertford. Broke up his marriage. You must remember!'

I put my cup carefully down on the saucer and looked at her in astonishment. The Hertfords were the leading county family, and although they no longer lived at Hertford Manor, which they had had to give to the National Trust, their name was still evocative of bygone glories to people of Mrs Dudley's generation, and, indeed, to mine as well. Jamie was their adored eldest son, a golden boy, wonderfully handsome and with immense charm – as young girls we were all, more or less, in love with him. He had for us the sort of glamour that an actor or a television personality has for the young today. I had known him quite well because my brother, Jeremy, who was six years older than me, was at boarding school with him (being the only son, he was, of course, sent to Clifton, my father's old school) and they saw each other a lot in the holidays. Sometimes they would let me tag along with them when they went out rough-shooting or fishing. I remember stifling my misery at the sight of the pathetic furry bodies, or the poor gasping fish, because I was full of the glory of being with Jamie and I knew just how envious my contemporaries would be. They also went hunting together – Colonel Hertford was the Master for several seasons. I was never keen on horses (frightened of them, if I am honest) so I could only admire Jamie and Jeremy from afar as they rode off, like two young gods. They did their National Service in the same regiment, but Jeremy was sent to Cyprus and never came back – shot one hot morning on the road to Limassol. Jamie didn't go abroad, and when he came out of the army, he married Alison Freemantle, and everyone had said how suitable, because their families were connected in some way.

Alison was only seventeen, a fair, pretty, gentle child, who worshipped Jamie. But, alas, in the army he had acquired a taste for drink and gambling, and his youthful high spirits and sense of adventure had turned to recklessness and uncertain temper. They settled at the Home Farm, but Jamie had not cared for farming, preferring to spend his days hunting and horse-dealing and riding in point-to-points so wildly that I could hardly bear to watch him pushing his horses ruthlessly over the fences. Alison, poor girl, couldn't really cope with him and so she withdrew more and more into herself, devoting her time to her two children, a boy and a girl. On the rare occasions when I met her, she had developed a sort of plaintive, complaining manner, which must have made Jamie even more bad-tempered and impossible to live with.

After a few years they had moved out of the district. The Home Farm was sold and there were a lot of debts – his father was dead by then, but I think he'd run through most of the family money, apart from an annuity of his mother's which he couldn't get his hands on. I knew that he and Alison were divorced, because a little while afterwards she was back in Taviscombe, more subdued than ever, living with her parents and the little girl. I heard that the boy had stayed with his father, and was surprised that Jamie could be bothered with a child.

'When did he marry Lee then?' I asked.

'Oh, she got hold of him when he left Taviscombe and went down to North Devon. I think she came from somewhere near Instow. Then, after the divorce, she married him.'

'But how do you know all this?'

Mrs Dudley tossed her head slightly. 'Poor Mrs Hertford and I have always been great friends.'

This was certainly news to me. In the old days Mrs Dudley had certainly not moved in county circles. For that matter, neither had we. It was only Jerry and Jamie being at the same school that had given us a limited entrée into the charmed circle. I supposed that after the financial troubles and Jamie's general disgrace after his father's death, Mrs Dudley had seized her chance to 'take up', as she would have said, 'poor Mrs Hertford'.

'Where is he living now?' I asked.

'Oh, still in North Devon. He has a sort of market garden – can you imagine such a thing! – near, now *where* is it . . . Georgeham! That's right. I believe he's in quite a bad way. Though of course Mrs Hertford never says as much, she's still very loyal, but I can always read between the lines. So,' she finished triumphantly, 'what do you think of that!'

I was still reeling from all this unexpected information and made no reply.

'Now, you really must have a piece of Elsie's Victoria sandwich – you always used to like it so much. No one can make a Victoria sandwich like Elsie.' She spoke as if she was personally responsible for the excellence of the Victoria sandwich.

'No thank you – I really couldn't manage another crumb! It was all quite delicious.'

'Well, I expect you have to watch your figure. Like poor Rosemary – I'm always telling her she should go on a proper diet, but I'm afraid she's really letting herself go nowadays. I said she ought to try that new little man I've found in Taunton for her next perm, but she said she can't be bothered. Do you know,' she said in a shocked tone, 'she may be my own daughter, but I do believe she has never had a proper manicure in her entire life!'

I hastily hid my unvarnished, garden-stained nails in my lap and gave a non-committal murmur. I felt I should tackle Mrs Dudley about the extraordinary information she had just given me.

'You will be telling all this – about Lee and Jamie Hertford – to the police, won't you?'

She gave me a cold look.

'Certainly not. I wouldn't dream of letting that self-opinionated young man of Jilly's know all poor Mrs Hertford's business!'

'But Mrs Dudley, they ought to know – it might help them with their enquiries.'

'You are not suggesting, I hope, that any of the *Hertfords* had anything to do with this unsavoury affair?'

'Well, no, not necessarily – but it might be relevant in some way.'

79

'And just suppose the *Echo* got hold of it. How do you think Mrs Hertford would feel, having all her private affairs splashed across the front page?'

Since Mrs Dudley was an avid reader of any sort of local gossip, I felt this was a bit thick.

'Well, I suppose Mrs Hertford may be going to the police herself, when she hears the news.'

Mrs Dudley gave me a triumphant look. 'Oh, didn't you know – but, of course, how could you, I don't suppose you ever see the family nowadays – she's not in England at the moment. She always spends the worst part of the winter with her nephew in South Africa. He has a sugar – can it be? – plantation somewhere near Durban. Of course, he pays her air-fare, because I don't think she could possibly afford it now. His wife's a South African, but quite a nice girl I believe.'

I made another attempt to persuade Mrs Dudley that it was her duty to tell the police what she knew about Lee's background, but her stubbornness and snobbery made it very unlikely that she would do anything of the sort. So yet again – as in the case of Carol – I had been given information that the police might not have. I wasn't sure what I was supposed to do with either item.

I got to my feet and thanked Mrs Dudley for my splendid tea.

She shook my hand in both of hers and said, 'My dear Sheila, you know I always like to see old friends. The world is so full of dreadful things nowadays. I sometimes feel that I am an old, old woman who has outlasted her time.'

She paused, waiting for me to say that of *course* she wasn't old and that she would see us all out – but I rather meanly didn't. I simply said that it was nice to see her and that I hoped Rosemary would be better soon.

'Oh, she always seems to have something wrong with her – I really don't know about you young people. *I* don't know what it is to have a day's illness.' I remembered various occasions when Rosemary had been summoned to her mother's side for some trivial complaint that Mrs Dudley had decided was terminal, but made no comment, merely saying goodbye and getting away as quickly as possible.

As I drove home I was in a state of total confusion. At the best of times a prolonged tête-à-tête with Mrs Dudley left me feeling drained and limp, and this, together with the amazing news I had just been given, made me quite incapable of coherent thought.

I put the car away, went into the house and busied myself with mindless household tasks. Tris and Foss, left alone all afternoon, demanded my attention. I let them both out into the garden and stood at the back door watching them idly in the twilight. Tris ran round and round in circles barking madly and making little darts at Foss who, feigning alarm, rushed up a tree. I groaned. It was an old beech tree with a smooth trunk, and although Foss could get up it perfectly easily he always forgot that he couldn't get down. He perched, as he always did, in the first fork, peering down forlornly and howling for help.

Resignedly, I went to the garden shed to get the step-ladder, praying that he would stay where he was and not go any further up. Fortunately the higher branches were swaying in the wind, so he stayed put until I gingerly climbed the steps and snatched him down. His claws dug into my shoulder and Tris jumped up and down round my feet at the bottom of the steps and I wondered aloud why I ever bothered with tiresome animals in the first place. Foss leapt down and rushed into the house, pursued by Tris, and they both sat hopefully in the kitchen, waiting for me to put away the steps and come and feed them.

All this activity cleared my mind, and when I finally sat down with the glass of sherry I felt I had really earned, I had decided what to do. I would go to Georgeham and see if I could find Jamie Hertford. At the very least I could tell him that his ex-wife was dead, and maybe he could tell me something about her that would help in some way to solve the mystery of her death. And – if I was absolutely honest with myself – I was very curious to see what Jamie looked like nowadays.

After supper I finally nerved myself to tell Charles what had happened. Because of the time difference I had to ring him at his office, which involved getting past a collection of strong-minded secretaries, so that when I finally got hold of him I was feeling decidedly on edge.

'Yes, Sheila,' he said, 'what is it? Have you any news?'

'Charles, look, I'm awfully sorry – it's very bad. Lee's dead.'

'Dead?' The single word sounded as lifeless as its meaning.

'She was murdered. I found the body.'

Through Charles's exclamations of shock and incredulity I tried to explain as simply and clearly as I could just what had happened.

'But how did you *know* she'd be there?'

'Charles, I *told* you – it was just a feeling I had
... no *reason*. I was still trying to find out for
you ... '

'Yes, I see ... '

There was a pause, and I had the impression that
Charles was working something out in his mind.
When he spoke again his voice was steadier.

'Look, Sheila,' he said, 'how about the police?
Have they been through the papers at her office?'

I was startled at this sudden business-like approach.

'I don't know – they hadn't this morning. They
just interviewed Carol – that's the girl who works
there – and looked through Lee's appointment
book, but that's all so far, I think.'

'Ah.'

There was another pause, and then Charles said,
'Actually, I didn't tell you everything last time. But
now Lee's dead – well, it makes a difference. You
see, I handed over a very much larger sum of
money, much more than I told you. There was
this deal ... '

'A property deal?'

'Yes. She'd got wind of this hypermarket development – she was buying up property in single lots
as my agent. Well, we stood to make a pretty good
killing ... ' The ineptitude of this phrase didn't
seem to strike him and he went on, 'It was all
very hush-hush – planning permission from the
local council and all that, it all had to be done
very carefully.'

Councillor Bradford, I thought suddenly. That
was her contact. But what was in it for him, and
why was he so anxious to see her, making those
visits to her flat? No wonder she didn't keep the
documents about *that* deal in the office.

'Well,' I said, 'I expect the police will find the papers soon enough – probably at her flat.'

'Yes, I suppose so. It's going to be a bit embarrassing.'

'Well,' I said sharply, 'there's nothing I can do about *that*.'

Surely Charles didn't expect me to break into Lee's flat and steal the papers, like some secret agent.

'Look, Sheila, my dear, this has been the most dreadful shock – I haven't really come to terms with it yet. I need time to think. I'll ring you tomorrow.' Then, as an afterthought, 'It must have been pretty awful for you.'

'Yes,' I said with restraint, 'it was, rather.'

'Well, Sheila dear, I'll ring you tomorrow. Or perhaps the day after – soon, anyway. And if you *can* find out what the police are doing, I'd like to know.'

As I put down the receiver my previous concern for Charles was replaced by irritation. It seemed to me that he was far more concerned about his wretched money than with the fact that the woman he was going to marry was dead. Well, perhaps that wasn't fair, he probably still hadn't taken in the fact that she actually was dead. And, I suppose, with someone like Charles one's business instincts always come to the fore, no matter what. Still, I felt slightly resentful. Had all his concern about Lee's disappearance really been because of his money? Did *he* think, as I had momentarily thought, that she had simply taken the money and gone? But as I recalled my talk with Lee that day, I couldn't doubt that she had been speaking the truth. She really had intended to marry Charles, I was quite sure. Her voice as she spoke of him had the quality of confidence and satisfaction that another woman can always recognise in such circumstances. Besides, Charles was rich and reliable. I had no idea what her second husband, the unknown Mr Montgomery, had been like, but certainly Charles would be a vast improvement on a gone-to-seed Jamie Hertford. I wondered how long that marriage had lasted.

Jamie . . . my thoughts returned to him. Ja . . . Jay! Of course, that was who she had been going to meet the day before she disappeared – it had to be. But why? What could she possibly want with him and why had she been so anxious to see him? Now there was a stronger reason than mere curiosity for me to go to Georgeham tomorrow.

Chapter Seven

I reached Georgeham about mid-morning the next day, having got myself lost in the narrow Devon lanes which run between high banks and which all look the same. I have absolutely no sense of direction. Peter used to be very patient with me but he never understood how anyone could *not* know which way to turn at a junction. ('But don't you see – that way will simply take us back the way we came!') Still, I got there eventually. It was a small place and I didn't think it would be too difficult to find out where Jamie lived. I had a choice really – I could enquire at the garage or at the post office. My tank was almost full so I opted for the post office.

There were several people in the post office, which was also the village shop. I took my place in the queue and settled down for a long wait. As purchases were made and local news exchanged, I looked around to see what I could buy. I was rather impressed by what they had. Presumably having decided that this was their best way of competing with the supermarkets in Barnstaple and Ilfracombe, the owners had laid in stocks of health and speciality foods. When I finally reached the counter I had quite a little collection of delicacies – smoked trout pâté and local goat's cheese, as well as some organically grown carrots.

As I paid for my purchases I asked, 'Can you tell me where I can find Mr Hertford's market garden?'

'Market garden?' The young woman behind the counter looked doubtful. 'Well, there's Mr Hertford up at West Lynch, but I don't know that you would call it a market garden – though I suppose he does grow some veg and things.'

'It sounds like him. Mr Jamie Hertford . . . '

'Oh yes, that's him. Lives up there with his son. Keeps bees, the son does, and a few goats. That's his cheese you just bought.'

'Can you tell me how to get there, please?'

West Lynch was apparently about a mile and a half out of the village, and she gave me directions which I repeated carefully after her. The other people, who had come into the shop after me and were waiting to be served, looked at me curiously, and I imagined the speculation there would be when I had gone.

It was a milder day, but damp and rather miserable. The countryside looked bleak and sodden. It wasn't a particularly picturesque part of Devon anyway – it all looked a bit run-down, and there seemed to be a lot of old tyres and rusting corrugated iron around in the farmyards. As I drove, I wondered just how I would approach Jamie – how I would get in, even – but to my relief, when I reached the turning to West Lynch, I saw a hand-written sign that said 'Farm Shop'.

I drove cautiously up the rutted, muddy track and drew up in front of a dilapidated barn, which also bore a 'Farm Shop' sign. There was a small tractor in the yard and bits of what I took to be agricultural machinery in varying stages of decay. Behind the barn I could see a horse-box and a very old Land Rover. The house was stone-built – unusual for this part of the country – square, grey and ugly. It looked as if it would be cold and uncomfortable. Behind the house and some other out-buildings there was a walled garden, with rows of rather frost-bitten vegetables, and beyond that a field with two horses. Four goats were tethered in a corner of the yard and I hoped they were secure, since I have never entirely trusted goats after having been charged by a particularly ferocious one when I was a child.

I got out of the car and went into the barn. Inside, there were trestle tables with boxes of apples and washed vegetables. Someone had obviously tried very hard to make an attractive display. There were also pyramids of jars of honey – all labelled 'West Lynch Organic Honey' – and some goat's cheese, like that I had bought from the shop. At one end of one of the trestles there were some dried-flower arrangements, not very well done, and rather touching. I couldn't imagine that any of this was Jamie's handiwork. I also wondered who on earth they expected to drive up their muddy track for such a relatively meagre display of goods – especially at this time of the year.

There was a bell on the table with another hand-written sign that read 'Please ring'. I rang it vigorously, hardly expecting anyone to come, but a young man came in from the back and said in a quiet, almost timid voice, 'Can I help you?'

As he came into the light, I could see at once that it was Jamie's son. Physically, he was so like the Jamie I remembered, the same features and the same colouring, but without the dash and vivacity of his father he looked like a pale, pastel copy of an oil-painting.

I smiled reassuringly. 'I'd like some honey, please.'

'Clear or set?'

'Clear, please. With such lovely local honey I like to have it on yoghurt.'

He reached over to get a jar and carefully re-arranged the pyramid.

I moved along to the dried flowers and picked out a rather untidy posy.

'These are nice,' I said.

He flushed and looked pleased.

'Did you do them?' I asked.

'Yes. It's the first year I've grown them and I'm not very good at arranging them yet.'

'They're lovely colours,' I said, 'yellow and white. I like statice, it doesn't drop bits all over every-thing.'

He smiled nervously. It was difficult to talk to him, he seemed very nervy – 'highly strung' Anthea would have said disapprovingly – so that it was rather like approaching a nervous animal whose confidence had to be won.

I paid him for the honey and the dried flowers, and then I said, 'I wonder – would it be possible to see your father?'

'My father?' He looked puzzled and rather wary.

'Yes. I used to know him – years ago – and I would love to say hello, if he's around.'

He hesitated and then said, 'Will you come through then?'

He led the way out of the barn and towards the house. As we came out into the daylight I saw that he was not as young as I had first thought. He was considerably older than Michael, in his thirties perhaps. I did some calculations in my head – yes, he might well be all of that. It was his manner that made him seem so much younger, the timidity and an almost child-like simplicity. I felt that for him everything was black and white, no shades of grey, as it is for a child.

He took me into the house through a side door which led into a narrow hall with an ochre and black tiled floor. I was right about the cold, it hit you quite palpably as you went into the house. He opened a door into what was presumably the sitting room and we went in. It was a large, square room which might have seemed cheerless but for the obvious care that had been taken with it. The furniture was shabby but meticulously polished, the curtains and the covers on the chairs were faded but newly laundered, and along both window-sills there were rows of flowering pot-plants. There was a good fire burning in the grate, and in an armchair to one side of the fireplace sat a man reading a copy of *Horse and Hound*.

'Dad' – the voice was even more hesitant – 'there's someone who wants to see you.'

The man looked up. It was Jamie Hertford. I don't quite know what I had expected. No, that's not quite true. I had had a picture of a Jamie, red-faced and run to fat, bloated almost, the result of the drink and the dissipated life – a sort of Henry VIII figure in breeches and riding boots, all the glory faded and gone. The reality was an even greater surprise. To begin with, he seemed to have shrunk. Jamie had never been tall exactly, but he had looked taller than he was because of his vigour and upright bearing.

This Jamie seemed positively short and very thin. His face was reddish brown, tanned to leather, more by the wind than by the sun. His features, which had been of an almost classical perfection, had sharpened – his nose, which was red-veined, seemed longer and more pointed, the line of his mouth was thin, and he now had a thick moustache, which was grey like his hair. Only the blue eyes were the same, though even they were now slightly red-rimmed and looked weak behind the reading glasses he was wearing.

I was struck by a moment of terrible sadness as I remembered my last meeting with the golden Jamie I had known. It was at a Hunt Ball, and Jamie and Jeremy had both been on leave at the same time. Although I was still only sixteen I had pestered my mother so much that she had agreed that I could go, and Jerry, with the kindness that was always the essential part of his nature, agreed to take me as his partner. I was in a daze of delight with my first grown-up ball dress. It had been made by my mother's dressmaker and was pale blue moiré taffeta, 'suitable' to my age, with the fashionable sweetheart neckline and puffed sleeves, but it did have a gloriously full skirt with a stiff net petticoat that made it stick out like a crinoline. So, although I did hanker for something black and strapless, I was very pleased with my appearance. It was one of those rare, totally magical evenings when everything miraculously lives up to your expectations. No one treated me as a child and I had a lot of partners – above all I had the wonderful feeling, so precious to an adolescent, of being accepted into the glamorous grown-up world. Hunt Balls usually end with the Gallop and I was just looking round for Jeremy, who had promised to dance it with me, when my wrist was seized by Jamie, who cried, 'Come on, young Sheila' and swept me into the dance. I had never seen him looking so splendid as that evening, his face flushed, his fair hair slightly dishevelled and his brilliant blue eyes glittering with excitement. I suppose, looking back now, he must have been rather drunk, but that didn't occur to me then; I was simply swept away by a wild feeling of exhilaration. As we whirled round and round the full skirt of my dress swung out and I was all the heroines in all the films I had ever seen and all the books I had ever read. I was totally and blissfully happy. I don't remember the dance finishing or going home, or anything; my memory stopped at that perfect moment.

I drew a deep breath and smiled at the man in the chair, who had half risen to his feet.

'Hallo, Jamie,' I said. 'I don't expect you remember me – it's Sheila Fulford, Jeremy's sister.'

He stood up and looked at me in a bewildered sort of way.

'Jeremy,' he said, 'Jeremy Fulford.' A look of pain crossed his face. 'Poor Jeremy – Cyprus, wasn't it? I remember now. Yes, of course I remember you. Little Sheila.'

He put out his hand and I shook it formally. The skin felt dry and rasping and the nails were broken and grimed from working out of doors.

'How are you?' he went on. 'You've met my boy Andrew I see.'

'Yes, indeed. I've just been buying some of his delicious-looking honey.'

'Yes, well, he does most of the work around here nowadays – bees and goats and vegetables and so on. We're thinking of getting some Jacob sheep

– wool, you know. He's been reading it up. Marvellous touch with animals. Horses too. That's all I
really do now. A bit of dealing, horse-transporting
sometimes. Getting old.'

I laughed. 'Aren't we all?' I said, and we exchanged
a few inanities about how time flew and it seemed
like only yesterday . . .

He didn't ask how I had found him after all
these years. It has always amazed me that men
– most men, anyway – are so incurious, hardly
ever questioning why things happen. My mother
would have said, in her acerbic way, that they are
so occupied with their own lives and thoughts that
they never bother to think of anyone else's. At any
rate, I was glad of Jamie's lack of curiosity.

I nerved myself to say what I had come to say.

'Jamie,' I said, 'I'm afraid I have some rather
bad news. Lee – your ex-wife – she's dead, she
was killed.'

He made no sort of movement, almost as if he
hadn't heard me, and there was complete silence,
broken suddenly by a sort of gulping sound from
Andrew. I turned to look at him. His face was red,
his eyes were blazing with excitement and he was
clenching and unclenching his hands. He faced his
father and almost shouted, 'Aren't you glad – she's
dead, she's gone, she can't hurt us any more! Say
you're glad – say it!'

'Andrew, stop that!'

'She's *dead*. It's what we wanted – we need never
see her again – never!'

'*Andrew*!' Jamie's voice was fierce and hard.
'You're hysterical. Pull yourself together – you
don't know what you're saying!'

Andrew flinched as if from a blow, more from

the tone of voice than from the actual words. He began to cry. It was a pitiful sight, and I turned away and looked out of the window. Then I heard Jamie say gently, 'It's all right, old chap. It was a shock, wasn't it. It's all *right*. Now, you just go and get some coffee for us all, that's what we need now, a nice cup of coffee.'

I heard the door close as Andrew went out of the room, and, reluctantly, I turned to face Jamie.

Chapter Eight

He was standing in front of the fireplace, still holding the copy of *Horse and Hound*.

'I'm sorry about that,' he said. 'As you see, Andrew
gets a bit overwrought sometimes. Do, please, sit
down.'

I sat in the other armchair and faced him across
the fireplace.

'I'm sorry if my news was a bit of a shock,'
I said.

'A shock?' He seemed to consider this. 'Yes, I
suppose it was.'

There was another silence. Then he said, 'I suppose you're entitled to some sort of explanation.'

He got up and went into the hall and I heard
him call to Andrew.

'Leave the coffee for a bit, old man. Go on out
and finish mucking out Rajah's stable, will you –
thanks, that's splendid.'

He came back into the room and sat down again.
'He'll be better with the horses for a while – that
always calms him down if he gets upset.'

'He seems very fond of animals,' I said, trying
to ease the conversation along.

'Yes – he's a marvel with horses – can ride anything – has a sort of sympathy with them, I suppose.

Yes, well, I was going to explain, though it's hard to know where to begin.'

'When were you and Lee divorced?' I asked.

'Divorced?' He looked at me blankly. 'We're not divorced. Lee is – was – still my wife.'

'But what about Mr Montgomery?'

'They weren't married. I suppose I'd better tell you about it from the beginning.' He leaned back in his chair. 'You know that Alison and I split up when the kids were small. All my fault, I led her the hell of a dance, poor girl. She went back to her parents and took the children with her. But Andrew – he was about seven – wouldn't settle. He'd always been very devoted to me, used to follow me about like a little dog, even though I was a rotten father. But, anyway, he had these screaming fits and things so he came back to me – I was living the other side of Exeter then – and Charlotte stayed with Alison. Poor little creature, he didn't have much of a life – I was involved with Lee by that time, and then we got married and bought this place. We led a pretty rackety life – you know, too much drink, too many parties, too many horses coming in last. Andrew had to fend for himself most of the time.'

'Didn't Lee like children?'

'She liked them to like *her*, and when there were other people around she always made a fuss of Andrew, so that everyone said how marvellous she was with him. She was never cruel to him, but she just couldn't be bothered most of the time. She used to tease him, and, poor child, he rose to the bait every time. And then she laughed at him – it was thoughtlessness really, but it hurt Andrew just as much as real cruelty would have done. I used to laugh at him too, before I realised . . . '

Oh Charles, I thought, what a lucky escape your children have had!

'Anyway,' Jamie continued, 'we went on like that for quite a while – things went from bad to worse and there wasn't much money. We were both fairly drunk a lot of the time – it was all pretty squalid. Lee used to go off occasionally with some chap or other, and then one time when she was driving back from London she had an accident. Quite serious, court case and everything. She was fined and lost her licence for a year. That seemed to sober her up. She seemed to pull herself together and decided she wanted a lot more out of life than I could offer her. That's when she took up with Ralph Montgomery. He was years older than she was – late sixties I should think – a retired business man, pots of money. He was absolutely besotted with her and set her up in a flat in Exeter.'

'Why didn't they get married?'

'Oh, he was married already. Didn't want a divorce because of his children. It didn't seem to worry Lee, she just called herself Montgomery.'

'Why didn't you divorce her?'

'The whole thing shook me up – that and too much drink. I had a sort of breakdown. Alison tried to take Andrew away, but he wouldn't go. He was in his early teens by then and he pulled me through – put up with me, nursed me, generally looked after me. It was quite extraordinary. Gradually we built up something here – a sort of market garden, Andrew's bees and goats, my horses. We just about manage to break even. He works so hard, that boy, all the hours God sends. But I think he's happy now. At least, he was . . . '

'What happened?'

'Lee – she got in touch again, after all those years. She said she wanted a divorce. I thought she was going to marry Montgomery, but he had died. Though he had set her up in an estate agency business – in *Taviscombe*, of all places! I wondered if my mother knew . . . '

'Oh yes,' I said, 'people have long memories in places like Taviscombe.'

'Anyway, she was going to marry someone— '

'Charles Richardson,' I said. 'He's an old friend of mine. Do you remember Fred Richardson? He was a bank manager – his son. Charles works for a big multi-national and lives in America. Lee was selling his mother's house – that's how they met.'

'A lot of money?'

'Yes.'

'The *bitch*,' he said violently. 'She didn't need the money, then . . . '

'What do you mean?'

'She rang me up and said she had to see me. She wanted a divorce and she wanted a settlement.'

'What sort of settlement?'

'We bought this place in our joint names. I couldn't possibly raise the money to buy her out. I would have had to sell up, after all the work we'd put in – the one place where Andrew feels safe.'

He gripped the arms of his chair; then, recovering himself, he said quietly, 'The awful thing is, she spoke to Andrew first – on the phone.'

'What happened?'

'Oh, just as usual, she couldn't resist teasing and tormenting him. She said she was coming back, and that it would all be just like it used to be . . . '

'Oh, *no*, the poor boy!'

He gave me a grateful look. 'It was terrible, he

went off for three days – took one of the horses and just went off. I was dreadfully worried, anything might have happened with him in that state.'

'Where did he go?'

'I don't know – he came back eventually because of Rajah – the horse. There was no feed for him out on the hills. Andrew was starving and exhausted. He'd been sleeping rough, in that awful frost, too. It took the best part of a week to get him back to normal again. It wasn't just the physical illness, I had to convince him that Lee was never coming back again – no matter what I had to do to prevent it.'

'Did you meet her?'

'Yes, while Andrew was missing – I'd said I'd see her at Wringcliff Bay – miles from anywhere. For some reason she was very anxious not to be seen with me. I was half beside myself with worry, but I had to see her. I had to tell her that she wasn't going to wreck our lives again.'

'What happened?'

'She said she wanted a divorce as quickly as possible – and the money from the house. She said if she got it she would go right away, but if not she'd have to come back to us . . . I said I'd find the money somehow but I needed time. I pleaded with her. I took hold of her arm and tried to make her see how she would be destroying Andrew as well as me if we had to sell up. But she wouldn't listen. She shook my arm off and said that I must do the best I could and she'd be in touch again, very soon. Then she went away.'

'Oh, Jamie . . . '

'I sat in the Land Rover for a long time trying to think what to do, but all I could think of was Andrew. So I came back here and then, the next day, thank God, Andrew came home, and for about a week I was so busy looking after him that I had barely time to think of anything else. And then, as time went by, and I didn't hear from Lee, I began to think that she'd changed her mind. I let myself hope, well, you know, the way you do, that she'd changed her mind, or something . . . '

'Charles – the man she was going to marry – thought she *was* divorced. I suppose that's why she didn't want anyone to see you together.'

'I suppose so . . . If only I'd *known* that she was going to marry a rich man . . . there would have been no *need* . . . '

His voice trailed away and he sat staring into the fire. We sat in silence for some time and I too watched, as if mesmerised, the ash falling from the burning logs in the grate. There was a lot I felt I should be asking Jamie, but I couldn't bring myself to ask questions just then.

After a while he raised his head and said, in quite a different tone of voice, 'But what about you? What have you been doing all these years?'

I told him about my marriage and about Peter's death, using the form of words I had evolved to spare myself thinking about the hurt, and about Michael and about my 'work' and my busy life.

'Poor Sheila,' he said, and with a perception the old Jamie would never have had, he added, 'We all build a pearl around the grit, as best we can. It takes a while, but it's worth it in the end.'

'Yes,' I said. 'I am beginning to find that.'

He looked at his watch. 'Will you stay to lunch? We usually only have a bit of bread and cheese – Andrew's goat cheese, it's very good – but you are very welcome.'

I got to my feet. 'It's awfully kind of you, but I ought to be getting back . . . ' I picked up the honey and dried flowers that I had laid on the floor at my feet. 'I shall look forward to trying this lovely honey.'

He led me out into the hall and opened the front door.

'Say goodbye to Andrew for me,' I said. 'I won't disturb him now if he's busy.'

'Yes, I will. And, Sheila,' he put his hand on my shoulder, 'please come and see us again. Andrew took to you – I could tell that – and I'd like you to see him when – well, when he's more himself.'

'Of course I will,' I said warmly. 'Perhaps I could bring Michael, when he's home from Oxford. Who knows,' I added, knowing that it could never be, 'they might become friends like you and Jerry were . . . '

'That would be nice.'

He stood beside me as I opened the door of my car, and when I drove away I could see him in my rear mirror, still standing where I had left him.

I somehow found my way back through the narrow lanes and on to the main road. What I needed now was time to sit down and consider what I had learned. I really couldn't allow my mind to sift through the extraordinary information and impressions I had just received while I was still driving. I stopped at a pub and ordered a plate of hot, comforting shepherd's pie and an even more comforting gin and tonic.

So my first impression of Lee had been the right one. She really was an unspeakable sort of person. That meeting I had with her on the day we went to Plover's Barrow had lulled me into a sort of reluctant liking. But *that* was simply Lee exercising her charm to win my approval of her marriage to Charles, because she thought I still had some sort of influence with him. I wondered how many others she had charmed for just long enough to get what she wanted. Now, having seen what she had done to poor Andrew, I could no more have tolerated her than if I had seen her striking an animal.

It was very terrible, I thought, that the first really strong motives for Lee's murder I had come across should be there, in that pathetic little household. Certainly Jamie had every reason to hate Lee and to want her dead. The break-up of all he had laboriously built, his own life and, even more, the precarious happiness of Andrew, all depended on the greedy whim of this woman. I could hardly find it in my heart to blame him if he *had* killed her. And then there was Andrew, who saw things as a child might see them, who was so horrified when he thought that Lee was coming back to torment them that he had run away. Where? *He* wouldn't think of it as murder. Jamie and Andrew – each would have killed for the other, with no more thought of any moral prohibition than a hunted animal would have when it turned on its pursuers.

'Would you like some coffee?' The young man from behind the bar came and removed my plate. The pub was empty, and he was disposed to stop and chat.

'Not much doing at this time of the year, even though we are on the main road. Not at lunch-time, that is. Evenings, now, we have Country and Western – they come from miles around, as far as

Plymouth sometimes, when it's something special. We got a good one on Saturday' – he indicated a large poster on the wall among the reproduction horse-brasses and hunting horns – 'Chuck Wayne and the Waggoners – they're great!'

I indicated my interest in all things Western by a little murmur and said that yes, please, I would like some coffee. He went away and I continued my brooding. I wondered if anyone else in Taviscombe, apart from Mrs Dudley, knew about Lee and Jamie. Obviously Rosemary didn't, or she would certainly have said something. But in a small town like Taviscombe there would always be somebody who would tell the police all about it, and *they* would not have the sentimental scruples I had about questioning Jamie very sharply about his movements and motives, and those of Andrew, on the day that Lee was murdered. No doubt when they went through Lee's papers they would find her marriage certificate and other things that would lead them to that little smallholding. I drove home slowly, worried and confused, wanting to do what was right, but reluctant to hurt those who seemed so vulnerable. When I got back I laid down my purchases on the kitchen table. The bunch of dried flowers had come undone and the fragile, papery blossoms spilled on to the floor. Foss batted one gently with his paw and looked at me enquiringly, but I had no answer.

For the rest of the day I tried to put the whole thing to one side. I cooked the animals' fish and made my supper and carefully watched nothing but soap operas and situation comedies on the television. I made a cup of tea and went up to bed, but my mind began churning about again, so I took up my familiar, blue-bound copy of *Pillars of the House* and lost myself, at last, in the myriad complexities of the Underwood family, until the small print caused my eyes to close and I finally fell asleep.

Chapter Nine

I woke up early the next day, which was just as well, because, not surprisingly, I'd forgotten I'd promised to make a cake for the Help the Aged Bring and Buy sale, which was being held that morning. I quickly threw together a sponge, but alas, when it had finished cooling on the wire rack, it looked decidedly lop-sided. I put an extra lot of jam filling in it and strewed the top liberally with icing sugar and hoped that nobody would notice. Needless to say, it didn't escape Marjorie Fraser's eagle eye.

'Oh dear – it seems to have sunk a bit,' she said, examining it critically.

'What a *cheek*!' Rosemary said indignantly as Marjorie moved away to supervise the making of the coffee. '*She* can't make cakes at all!'

'No,' I agreed, 'but she did bring those marvellous bowls of hyacinths. Did you see, all coming out at once and every single one the same size? I wish I knew how she did it.'

'I expect she speaks to them sharply,' Rosemary said acidly.

Then the doors of the church hall were opened and there was the usual scrum round the cake and jam stall, which soon looked as if it had been attacked by a swarm of locusts. Even my despised sponge was snapped up, by an elderly man in a deerstalker and a bright blue anorak. As I tidied away the paper plates that the cakes had been on and pushed to the front of the stall the remaining two jars of bramble jelly, I wondered if I should tell Rosemary about my visit to Jamie. My instinct was to keep it to myself. The fewer people who knew about his connection with Lee the safer he would be, and Rosemary could never keep a thing like that to herself. It was, indeed, very fortunate that Mrs Dudley hadn't said anything about it to her daughter. But I could understand that she wouldn't want anything to diminish the grandeur of the Hertford family in Rosemary's eyes, now that *she* could claim Mrs Hertford as a friend. Telling me was different. Jeremy had been Jamie's friend – she had always resented that – so she wouldn't scruple to pass on to me anything that might denigrate Jamie. I marvelled at the complexities of the English class system that could produce such fine degrees of snobbery! So perhaps I shouldn't tell Rosemary. But I dearly wanted to tell someone, and I knew that Rosemary would be as astonished as I was at the transformation in Jamie's appearance and in his life-style. The hall finally emptied, and Rosemary and I went into the small, inconvenient kitchen to wash up the coffee cups.

'I'll wash, shall I?' Rosemary asked. She looked at the plastic washing-up bowl and made a face. 'This really needs a good *scrub*. Oh well, never mind, pass me those cups will you.'

She started to talk of Lee's death and how upset Charles would be.

'Well, I don't know ... ' I said slowly. 'He'll get over it and he's well out of it, if you ask me.

Lee really wasn't at all a nice person.' That was the understatement of the year, but there was no way I could go into details without telling Rosemary too much.

'Yes, I suppose so. I didn't like her myself, but she might have suited Charles – he always liked his females to be sharp and rather glamorous. And, you never know, she wasn't *that* old – they might have had children— '

'Women like that don't *want* children,' said a harsh voice behind us. 'And heaven forbid that they should ever have any!'

We turned round in astonishment to see Marjorie Fraser standing behind us.

'They're too greedy and self-centred,' she said abruptly.

We were disconcerted by this interruption, and simply stood there, Rosemary with a dripping dish-cloth in her hand and me with a cup half-way into the cupboard. Marjorie's gaze swept over us disapprovingly.

'Those tea-towels could do with a good boil,' she said, and went out, banging the door behind her.

'*Well!*' said Rosemary at last.

'Why on earth should she go on about Lee like that?' I asked.

'I don't know. She can't have known her at all well – I mean, *would* she? They couldn't have anything in common. Perhaps she bought her house from Country Houses when she first moved here. I can't think how else they would have met.'

'I think it was something to do with children,' I said, and my thoughts turned to Andrew. Had Marjorie somehow heard about him? She moved in the same horsy set that Jamie used to belong to. Word might have filtered through; they were a gossipy lot.

'She's fond of children,' said Rosemary grudgingly, 'I know that. She does a lot with Riding for the Disabled, Anthea told me. I suppose she didn't have any children of her own, perhaps she couldn't. Sad to be left a widow with no children.'

'Yes,' I said.

Rosemary turned to me quickly. 'Well, you've got Michael, and he's super and very fond of you . . . But even if you were all alone I bet you wouldn't be all sour like Marjorie!'

'Who knows what I'd be like?' I said seriously. 'Children do make a difference . . . '

'Don't I know it,' Rosemary said, her mind darting off, as it so often did, in quite another direction. 'Did I tell you, Jilly and Roger are going to buy a house! A joint mortgage. Honestly, I *daren't* tell Mother, she'll go on and on about what will the building society think about them not being married!'

'Good for them,' I said. 'I like Roger. Jilly's very lucky. And if they're buying a house together it sounds as if it's turning into a stable relationship.' I tried not to put the phrase in inverted commas. 'What does Jack think about it?'

'Oh, he's all for it. He likes Roger too. He thinks they'll get married sooner or later so why make a fuss. You know what Jack's like – very *laissez-faire*! I'm the one who worries all the time.'

'Don't we all,' I said. 'Children!' And some of us have more to worry about than others, I thought, my mind going back to Andrew again.

Rosemary wrung out the dishcloth and draped it over the washing-up bowl, while I, mindful of

Marjorie's remark, put the damp tea-towels in my shopping bag to take them home to wash.

'It was a bit much,' Rosemary said, 'Marjorie butting in like that on a private conversation!'

'Well,' I said cattily, 'I don't suppose she'd let a little thing like good manners stop her if she had something she wanted to say!'

When I got home I picked up the local paper, which had been delivered that morning, and took it into the kitchen to read while I was having a sandwich and a cup of coffee. I spread it open on the kitchen table, and the first thing that caught my eye was a photograph of Councillor Bradford, making a presentation to a council worker who was retiring after thirty years' loyal service.

Now I came to think of it, I was really rather confused as to exactly *what* Lee's property deals had all been about. Philip Bradford had presumably approached her about buying up property when he heard of the proposed hypermarket development, and it would have to be done in someone else's name so that he wouldn't fall under suspicion. Well, it seemed that she *had* bought up the property, but in Charles's name. A double-cross, in fact. Bradford wouldn't be able to make a fuss because he wouldn't want it known that he had acted illegally as a councillor, so he had no come-back. But did he know yet what Lee had done? Had she gone on stringing him along, right up to the time she had been killed? If so he must be quite anxious – even more anxious than Charles was – to know what papers the police had found. I wondered how I could find out exactly who knew what.

Foss, who hated ttto be ignored, leapt on to the

table and walked deliberately over the paper, his long crooked tail waving in my face.

'All right,' I said resignedly, 'come on then.'

Leaving my half-finished cup of coffee, I cut up some ox liver for him. Tris, hearing the saucer being put down on the floor, came rushing into the kitchen demanding food as well. I wondered, not for the first time, how anybody ever got anything done when they had animals or children around.

When I came to take Tris for his walk it was brilliantly sunny. There was no wind but it was intensely cold, the sort of cold that seems to bite into the very marrow of your bones. I got Tris ready, putting on his fleece-lined plaid dog-jacket, of which we are both rather ashamed, but he is getting on a bit now and needs the extra warmth. The same might also be said about me, so I put on the dreadful old sheepskin coat that I keep only for dog-walking, my fur-lined boots and gloves and a sheepskin hat with ear-flaps that tie under the chin. This is a relic of Peter. We called it Nanook of the North, and Michael and I used to threaten to refuse to go out with him when he wore it. Nowadays I am grateful for the warmth and no longer care about its eccentric appearance. Finally I wound my old college scarf around my neck and the bits of my face exposed to the biting air, so that practically only my eyes were left uncovered.

With a slightly rolling gait, because of all my cumbersome clothing, I made my way down to the sea to let Tris have a run along the beach. The sky was a glorious pale blue and the sea almost translucent. As we walked along the sand I saw that the little pools left by the tide were already silver with ice – the temperature must have dropped very suddenly. Tris ran wildly about, making little dashes at seagulls, then suddenly stopping to investigate a piece of driftwood or seaweed. The air was so cold and sharp it was like breathing in broken glass, so I buried my nose in my scarf and tried to generate a little warm air. I was leaning against the old break-water for a short rest before turning back for home when a voice behind me said accusingly, 'I didn't recognise you, all bundled up like that.'

It was, of course, Marjorie Fraser, apparently in a better temper, exercising her golden cocker spaniel. She, of course, was neatly and suitably dressed for the cold weather in a Barbour jacket, cord breeches, Newmarket boots and a tweed hat.

'Oh, hello Marjorie – hasn't it got *cold* all of a sudden! No more hunting again if this goes on, I suppose?'

'No, it's been a rotten season – ground's either been like iron or a beastly quagmire.'

In the bright open air her face looked worn and very lined, so that I felt impelled to ask, 'Are you all right? You do look tired.'

'Oh – well, yes, I am a bit. I was up most of the night with Satin – that's the chestnut mare. A bad cough – I shall have to get Hawkins in to have a look at her if she's no better tomorrow.'

'I'm so sorry.'

Tris and the spaniel were engaged in a joyful game with a piece of driftwood, taking it in turns to toss it in the air and then both rushing after it barking madly. I regarded them fondly.

'Aren't they sweet?' I said.

'That Westy of yours is getting too fat,' she said critically. 'You'll have to put him on a high protein diet.'

There was a short silence while I swallowed my resentment but acknowledged the truth of what she said. It was very still and peaceful; we were the only people on the sands. There is a lot to be said for the seaside in winter.

On an impulse I turned to Marjorie and asked, 'Have you ever come across Jamie Hertford?'

She had been looking at the dogs, but her head jerked round and she regarded me sharply.

'Why do you ask?'

'I just wondered – you're both horsy, and hunt and so forth.'

'Yes. As it happens, I do know him,' she replied stiffly. 'As you say, we occasionally meet out hunting.'

'Have you met Andrew, his son?'

'Yes.' It was a barely acknowledged affirmative.

'Poor boy, he's terribly nervy . . . '

'How do *you* know them?' she asked me, almost accusingly.

'Jamie is an old friend,' I said evasively. 'He used to be at school with my brother.'

She seemed to relax slightly and I couldn't resist probing a little.

'Did you know that he was married to Lee Montgomery?'

She had turned away so that I couldn't see her face, but I could sense that she was very tense.

'That woman!' she said.

'She treated them both very badly I gather.'

'The world is well rid of her – she was . . . '
Marjorie was clenching and unclenching her hands, just as Andrew had done. The dogs suddenly rushed towards us, nearly knocking me over in their excitement.

'Tessa!' she called. 'Heel!' The dog ran obediently over and sat patiently beside her. The tension of the moment was broken.

'She certainly seems to have been pretty unpleasant,' I said inadequately. 'Jamie and Andrew have built a very peaceful little world without her. I can't get over how Jamie has changed.'

'He's been marvellous,' she said with a quiet intensity. She obviously knew much more about their lives than she was prepared to admit to me. '*He* devotes his life to that boy. *He* knows what it is to make sacrifices for one's child.'

She seemed about to say more, but her face suddenly flushed and she bent down to clip the dog's lead on to its collar.

Well! I thought. So that's it! The old Hertford charm was still there. Marjorie might not have admitted it, even to herself, but it was obvious to me that she was in love with Jamie.

Chapter Ten

Over the weekend I tried to put everything else out of my mind and get on with some work. I had to finish a study I was doing of Mrs Oliphant's *Salem Chapel*. It was for a collection of essays on the nineteenth-century novel, to be published in honour of the eightieth birthday of a distinguished literary critic, so that I had a very definite deadline and really had to finish it by the following week. I worked hard, stopping only to get myself snack meals and – more important – keep Foss and Tris provided with full saucers, so that by Sunday evening I had more or less finished. There were a couple of points I had to check, and as Taviscombe Public Library, although it is excellent for so small a town, doesn't run to a set of the *Dictionary of National Biography*, I decided that I would have to go to Taunton on Monday morning to consult the one there.

I made an early start and had a very satisfactory couple of hours checking the details I needed in the *DNB*, with all those side-trackings into that splendid publication that I can never resist. It was still only about midday, so I decided to go along to the Brewhouse Theatre to see if I could get a seat for *The Gondoliers* which the local operatic group were doing in a few weeks' time. Gilbert and Sullivan are immensely popular down here and I knew it would be pretty well booked out, but one of the few advantages of going to the theatre on your own is that you can often get a single ticket.

As I was carefully picking my way through the crowded car park I came face to face with Roger.

'Sheila! How extraordinary – I was going to ring you today.'

'Oh,' I said warily.

'Just a few things I wanted to say – off the record, as it were. Look, are you busy just now?'

'I was just about to try and get a ticket for the G & S,' I said.

'Oh, yes, Jilly and I are going on the Friday. They're very good, aren't they. Really most professional. Why don't we have lunch, if you haven't got to rush back?'

'That would be lovely,' I said. 'I was planning to have lunch here anyway – the food is splendid, as I expect you know.'

We went into the foyer and I managed to get a single ticket for the Wednesday.

'I love *The Gondoliers*,' I said, 'although I *think* that *Iolanthe* is my favourite.'

'If I had to choose, I think mine would be *Patience*. Probably because that's the one I saw first.'

Chatting casually about Gilbert and Sullivan, Roger led me into the main area where stalwart volunteer ladies stood behind a hatch serving out very good pasta dishes or cold meats and salad. All the food was home-cooked and the puddings were especially noteworthy. It was very obvious how the little theatre made most of its profits. As we were early, the dining room wasn't too full, so that we were able to find a table tucked away in a corner.

115

'Oh, you've got that gorgeous chestnut and cream thing. I can never decide between that and the sherry trifle . . . '

I told him about my article on Mrs Oliphant and what the other essays in the *Festschrift* were to be, staving off the moment when I knew he would be talking about Lee's death.

After a while he said, 'I do hope that you've quite recovered from that awful shock.'

'Yes, thank you. And thank you for being so marvellous. I don't believe I really said anything at the time, but . . . '

'Just looking at a murder victim is a horrible thing,' he said. 'Something you never get used to, however many times it may happen to you in the course of the job. It's the knowledge that somebody has done that to another human being.'

'I remember thinking – who could have hated her so much? That was dreadful.'

'There is no excuse for taking the life of another person.'

This flat statement, strangely echoing Mrs Dudley's 'Right is right and wrong is wrong', brought me up sharply.

'I agree with you, of course—'

'Why didn't you tell me about Jamie Hertford?'

'I honestly didn't know at the time. That is, of course I knew *him*, years ago when I was a child, he was a school-friend of my brother's. But he went away and we lost touch. So I never knew that he was married to Lee. Strangely enough, it was Mrs Dudley who told me. She knows Jamie's mother.'

'Jilly's *grandmother*! Did Rosemary know as well?'

'No, Mrs D. had her own inscrutable reasons for

not telling anybody. She only told me to score a snobbish point about my not knowing The Family (the Hertfords used to be practically lords of the manor, you know) as well as I thought I did!'

He laughed. 'That figures.' He finished off his lasagne and embarked on his creamy pudding. 'As you will have gathered, we found a marriage certificate and various letters among her effects at the flat. Did your friend Charles know about Jamie Hertford? He's local too, isn't he?'

'I'm sure he couldn't have. He actually thought she was divorced, presumably from the man Montgomery. *He* died – I expect you discovered that – and Lee was never married to him because she was still married to Jamie. Goodness, what a mess some people's lives are!'

'But you didn't know anything about it. Surprising for somewhere like Taviscombe.'

'It's really the previous generation – Mrs Dudley and her cronies – who kept up a spy system. We don't seem to have the time and the energy nowadays. Besides, Jamie went off to the other side of the county – into Devon, even, so interest would be proportionately less.'

'I went to see him, of course. He had to be told that his wife was dead. And I found that he knew already.'

I tore a bit off my bread roll and pulled it to pieces.

'I suppose, if I'm really honest, I was just curious to see what he looked like after all these years. I don't know if I can explain just how glamorous a figure he was when we were all young. Rich, handsome, well-born, with something of a reputation – just a hint of "mad, bad and dangerous to know". What young girl could resist! I expected

117

something quite different – all run–down and gone to seed. Instead – well, you've seen for yourself. Oh Roger, the pathos of it all!'

'And the son – would you think he's actually simple–minded?'

'No, not that. Child–like, I suppose, in some ways.'

'Obsessively devoted to his father, as his father is to him. There is nothing they wouldn't do for each other, wouldn't you say?'

I was glad for Jilly's sake that Roger was a sensitive and perceptive person, but just at that moment I would have preferred him to be the obtuse, plodding policeman of Mrs Dudley's imagining.

'But so *gentle*, Roger. Andrew is wonderful with animals, with plants. And Jamie – well, I simply can't believe ... ' My voice trailed away. We both had the same picture, I felt, of Jamie, goaded beyond endurance by Lee's vicious taunting, snatching up the knife. 'Roger,' I said briskly. 'I really don't know much about what you found at Plover's Barrow. Are you allowed to tell me? I feel so involved, as you can imagine. I really would like to know the actual *facts*. I suppose there's no chance of it having been a robbery of any kind?'

'No. Her handbag was there, with quite a large sum of money in cash – several hundred pounds, actually – and her cheque book and credit cards. No, not robbery.'

'And the knife?'

'Part of the stuff left behind in the house. There were several old knives and kitchen implements on the dresser. It was old and rusty, but it had a thin blade and did the job.'

I shivered. Then I thought of something that had been at the back of my mind for several days.

'Roger, I think that Lee must have gone to Plover's Barrow to meet a client.'

'What makes you think that?'

'She was wearing a suit, wasn't she, and high heels?'

'Yes.'

'Well, except when she was on business she always wore trousers and boots or flat shoes. That day we talked, she was saying how she hated skirts and never wore them except when she had to be done up for work or in the evening.'

'Yes. As a matter of fact I had come to something of the same conclusion. There was a dressing case in her car, and a suede jacket and a Harrods bag with trousers and a sweater and some other shoes. As far as we can judge, she wasn't at her flat the night before she was killed, so she must have taken her business suit and so forth with her to change for her appointment the next day.'

'Where can she have stayed?'

'That we will have to find out.'

'Certainly not with Jamie and Andrew – Jamie wouldn't have had her in the house! So you see . . .'

'All that doesn't alter the fact, I'm afraid, Sheila, that the two people – the only two people, as far as we know – who wanted Lee Montgomery dead were Jamie and Andrew Hertford. They have neither of them got an alibi. Andrew was off, riding over the hills in a highly emotional state. Heaven alone knows where he went. He can't, or won't, say. And his father had an extremely acrimonious interview with his wife in a very remote spot the day before she was killed, and no alibi at all for the day in question. He simply said he was out, looking for Jamie.'

'But if she was meeting a client at Plover's Barrow . . . '

'She could have arranged to meet Jamie Hertford there either before or after her business interview. She seemed to prefer meeting him in out of the way places.'

'I think that was because she didn't want Charles to know that she was still married – if anyone had seen her with Jamie something might have got back to him somehow.'

'But then, what about the client, whoever it was? It seems most likely that she was killed before he arrived. Something must have happened and he never showed up – only that one set of tyre tracks, remember.'

'It seems an extraordinary coincidence,' I said, unwilling to relinquish an unknown suspect, someone who wasn't Jamie or Andrew.

'True. But there is something else, something that I'm afraid points only too clearly to the Hertfords.'

'What's that?'

'Two things, actually. First of all, round the back of the house, where there's a gate that leads straight on to the moor. There were the hoof-marks of a lot of ponies.'

'Yes, I saw them that day – there was a little group of them standing round the gate.'

'Exmoor ponies are wild, of course, but among those hoof-marks there were marks of a horse that had been shod.'

'It couldn't have been an exception, I suppose – just one pony that had been shod for some particular reason?'

'I'm afraid not. In fact it wasn't a pony at all. The hoof-marks were definitely those of a horse, and quite a large horse at that. The imprints were much bigger and deeper than those of the ponies. And the other thing we found out confirms it. There was a shepherd, checking on his sheep across the valley. He noticed a man riding away from Plover's Barrow about midday. He was much too far away to give a proper description, but he certainly saw a figure on a horse. He says it was a large horse, possibly brown, though of course he can't say whether it was a bay or a chestnut or whatever. The rider was going away from him, round the edge of that wood, and making for the open moor.'

'But it would be much too far for Jamie or Andrew to come on horseback – it would have taken far too long.'

'Andrew went off the day before, remember, making for the moors. He would have just about reached that spot if he'd slept overnight in a barn or something, as his father thinks he did.'

'But how would he have known that Lee would be there?'

'He might have heard something when his father was talking to her on the phone.'

'I still don't think it's possible. But anyway, it would certainly be too far for *Jamie* . . . '

'There are such things as horse-boxes, you know, and the Hertfords do horse-transporting don't they? He could easily have left the horse-box in a lay-by up on the road. It wouldn't have been in any way remarkable. The hunt was out that morning and there are a lot of horse-boxes about on hunting days.'

I was silent for a while. Then I said, 'There's no sort of proof, is there? I mean, you can't match up the horse-shoes or anything?'

'No – that's not really possible. No proof. They can neither of them prove that they *weren't* there, but then we can't – so far – prove that they were.'

'I see.'

'I'm sorry, Sheila, but you must admit that they do seem to be the only people who have a real motive.'

I thought about Lee's property dealings.

'Have you investigated her business affairs? I'm sure far more people kill for money than for hate.'

Roger smiled. 'Inspector Dean is dealing with that side of things, being on the spot, as it were. Why? Do you know anything that we should know?' He looked at me quizzically.

'I don't actually *know* anything,' I said, wondering how I could divert the police's attention away from Jamie and Andrew without involving Carol and Charles. 'It's just that I got the impression, from what people have been saying,' I added vaguely, 'that Lee was involved in some sort of large property deal. It might be worth looking into.'

'It will be.' He put his elbows on the table and leaned forward sympathetically. 'I know how you feel about the Hertfords, Sheila. They have managed to salvage something very fragile from the wreckage of two lives. It would be very upsetting to have to smash it. But you have to face the fact that some-one's been killed – murdered. It isn't a fact that can be conveniently ignored, you know, just because the victim was unpleasant and the suspects are pathetic.'

'You're right, of course. Perhaps she was a spy,' I said hopefully, 'and was killed for the Secret Papers?'

'Heaven forbid,' he laughed. 'Things are compli-cated enough without having Special Branch breath-ing down my neck!'

I looked at the clock by the door.

'Goodness, look at the time. I must go. Thank you so much for my lunch, Roger, and for telling me what's going on. Can you let me know if there are any developments?'

If anything happened to Jamie or to Andrew the other would need a lot of support.

'Yes, I will. Keep your ears open for me, Sheila – the Taviscombe intelligence network probably hears a great many things that we don't.'

I promised that I would – though with certain mental reservations.

'I shall look forward to your essay on Mrs Oliphant.'

'If you're interested I'll send you a set of proofs – they usually let me have a couple.'

'Signed by the author, I hope.'

'Of course. Give my love to Jilly.'

We parted with friendly waves and I plunged into the Marks and Spencer food hall. As I packed various delicacies into my wire basket I tried to think of some way that I could find out *something* that would open up another line of police enquiry. A pack of American-style beefburgers decorated with the Stars and Stripes made me think of Charles. I might telephone him. He had been definitely evasive about his financial dealings with Lee. It wasn't that I wanted to throw him to the wolves to distract attention from Jamie and Andrew – he was an old dear friend. But he could look after himself, and they, poor things, certainly couldn't. And Charles was half a world away, across the Atlantic, while they were all too close to the scene of the crime.

Chapter Eleven

I did some calculations about the time difference and tried to phone Charles at his apartment before he left for work, but there was no reply. I gave it another hour and then tried his office. His secretary – Paula, I think she was called – with immense efficiency remembered my name from my previous calls to Charles.

'I'm so sorry, Mrs Malory,' she said. 'He isn't here right now. He had to go to Denver yesterday for about three days. He'll be travelling about, but I could give you the number of our Denver office . . . '

'No, really, it's not that urgent – I'll wait until he gets back.'

'He'll certainly be sorry to have missed your call. Just between ourselves, Mrs Malory, I think he gets a little homesick for England sometimes.'

'Yes, I think he does. Have you ever been to England yourself?'

'Oh, sure. Rob, that's my husband, and I, we were over just last spring. We did London, Stratford and Canterbury – it was really exciting. I said to Mr Richardson when I booked that trip for him to London in January, I sure do wish I was coming with you, to go to that wonderful Harrods sale – there's

TV advertisements for it over here you know. That really would be something!'

'January?' I asked.

'Sure. New Year's Day – but it was only a short trip, I guess.'

'I see. Well, thank you so much. If you could tell Mr Richardson that I called . . . '

'I surely will. Nice to speak with you, Mrs Malory.'

'Yes, thank you very much indeed.'

'My pleasure. Goodbye.'

I put the telephone down in a state of considerable bewilderment. Charles had said nothing about being in England at the beginning of January. Had he seen Lee then, and if so, where? In London? Surely he *couldn't* have been in Taviscombe – someone would have been sure to see him and word would get around. And *why* was he over here? And – most peculiar of all – why hadn't he told me about his visit when he telephoned about Lee? I was really beginning to get worried. Nothing seemed to make sense any more. My last telephone conversation with Charles had left me uneasy. I had the impression that he was holding something back and that there was something slightly discreditable that he didn't want me to know about. What *was* Charles up to?

The telephone rang. It was Anthea.

'Sheila? About Friday. Ronnie's cousin can't come, I'm afraid. He's got flu.'

I suppressed an unworthy exclamation of delight and said how sorry I was not to see him.

'But do come just the same, Sheila. I've invited Philip Bradford. You know him, he's on the District Council. Ronnie's met him quite a bit at various Rotary things and we owe him some hospitality! Actually, I was a bit worried about the numbers,

125

but it will be all right, we'll just be four, because his wife's away for six weeks visiting their daughter in Australia – she's just had her first baby and Moira, that's Moira Bradford, wanted to be out there with her— '

'That will be fine,' I broke into Anthea's usual monologue. 'The same time, then?'

'What? Oh, yes, seven for seven thirty.'

'Lovely. See you then.'

I replaced the receiver and said to Foss, who was sitting on the arm of my chair, '*Well*, Foss, what do you think of that? Isn't it splendid! Now I can see if I can find out anything from this Bradford man quite naturally. Isn't that lucky!'

But Foss was staring, in that disconcerting way that cats have, at some fascinating but invisible object in the far corner of the room, and paid no attention at all to what I was saying.

The following day brought a summons to the inquest. It was to be held at the local coroner's court in ten days' time. I felt very apprehensive at the idea of having to tell my story in public. My reasons for going out to Plover's Barrow would sound pretty feeble. And I would have to be careful what I said. For instance, I couldn't say that I knew Lee had an appointment there because Carol really shouldn't have shown me the appointment book and I didn't want to get her into trouble. Oh *what* a tangled web we weave . . . as Peter would have said.

Furthermore, I was not looking forward to seeing my name all over the front page of the *Echo*: 'LOCAL WOMAN FINDS MURDER VICTIM' or even, to make it a bit more classy, 'LOCAL WRITER FINDS BODY' – it would all be very distasteful. I was glad that Michael was away at Oxford, though when I had telephoned to tell him all about it, he had begged to be allowed to come home to 'do a bit of Sherlock Holmesing', an offer I had firmly declined.

I buttered myself another piece of toast, spreading the butter much thicker than usual, and topped it with some of Andrew's honey. Comfort eating, I told myself, and, indeed, I *did* find myself in need of comfort. I felt depressed and unsure and very much alone. If only Peter were here, I thought, he would know what to do. If Peter were alive, common sense told me, I would never have got mixed up in all this. After two years' grieving, you may think you've done with that first, sharp, painful misery, but it's always there, waiting for just such a moment as this, and then it comes back as strongly as ever, sweeping over you in waves.

I sat at the table for some time, not really thinking of anything but just having what my mother used to call 'a good wallow'. A ray of winter sun, shining on to the sideboard, made me get up and fetch a duster and that broke the mood, and I pulled myself together and did the washing up, thinking how lucky women were to have so many little tasks that simply had to be done, so that, in the end, cheerfulness did keep breaking in.

I still felt the need to talk to someone, so on impulse I telephoned Rosemary and invited her to tea, and that was a good thing because then I had to do some baking. I made a sponge (which, of course, rose perfectly this time, when it wouldn't come under Marjorie Fraser's critical gaze) and some shortbread and found a few snowdrops in the garden to put in my favourite little Victorian china basket. Spurred on by this burst of energy, and while the sun was shining, I bathed Tris. We both dislike this so much that I usually do it on the spur of the moment, when neither of us is expecting it, like this morning. I rubbed him dry and mopped up the kitchen floor, decided against using the hair-dryer on him because he hated the noise, and left him on a rug in front of the sitting-room fire looking clean but martyred. Foss, who had disappeared at the first sign of the plastic bath, suddenly materialised and sat on the window-sill delicately washing his paws and casting scornful glances at the poor creature who had to be washed by human beings.

Rosemary came nice and early, bringing with her a heavenly bunch of freesias.

'You sounded as if you needed cheering up,' she said, 'and no wonder when you come to think of it. You've had quite a time.'

'Roger bought me lunch at the Brewhouse yesterday,' I said. 'Wasn't that sweet of him? I *do* like him. Lucky Jilly!'

'Oh yes, certainly lucky Jilly. It's all working out very nicely. They've got their mortgage – it doesn't seem to matter whether you're married or not these days.'

'He wanted to talk to me about the case, of course. And, oh Rosemary, it is all so confusing! I simply *must* tell someone all about it . . . '

I cut us each a piece of sponge and poured the tea and, with occasional excited exclamations from Rosemary, I told her absolutely everything that I had found out, from whatever source.

'So you see how complicated it all is – you must promise not to tell anyone at all – even Jack.'

'Of *course*. Fancy Ma not telling me about Jamie Hertford and Lee!'

128

'You mustn't let her know that I told you, else she'll never speak to me again.'

'Lucky you!' Rosemary said.

'No, seriously. I wish you could see them though. It's an extraordinary set-up.'

'Do you think Marjorie Fraser is really in love with him?' Rosemary asked, fastening, as I knew she would, on the inessentials. 'Perhaps *she* murdered Lee,' she suggested frivolously, 'so that she could marry Jamie!'

'Poor Marjorie – I don't believe Jamie really notices her at all. They've shut the outside world out altogether, those two, that's the only way they can feel safe.'

'Goodness! When you *think*,' Rosemary exclaimed, 'how gorgeous he used to be. I was always frightfully jealous of you, being with him and Jeremy all the holidays ... '

'The trouble is, I do see how it must look to the police. I mean, you could hardly ask for a stronger motive, and then there's the bit about the horses.'

'I hate horses,' said Rosemary irrelevantly. 'Those awful big feet, and the way they toss their heads at you.'

'And then there's all this business about Charles and the property.'

'Oh well – you know what Charles is like about business!'

'Yes, but he's never been mixed up in anything shady.'

'I suppose you get pretty ruthless working for a multi-national, whatever it is he does.'

'I've never known exactly – something about petro-chemicals.'

'Well, there you are then.'

'Yes,' I said doubtfully, 'but it *is* rather different from land speculation in the heart of the West Country. I suppose it's *legal*, but definitely sharp practice, wouldn't you say?'

'Well, *that* wouldn't surprise me about horrible Lee,' Rosemary declared, her mouth full of shortbread. 'I never liked her, from that first moment when Charles introduced us. Nor did you.'

'No – but she did have a sort of charm. You'd never have guessed that she was so absolutely foul and cold-bloodedly cruel.'

'And greedy! I mean, she was going to have all Charles's money ...'

'And all the money they were going to make on this development thing ...'

'Yes. And *still* she wanted poor Jamie's little bit as well.'

'I wonder how she got hold of the news of that development. Do you think this man Bradford approached her?'

'He's a slimy toad,' Rosemary said vigorously. 'Jack says he's been in on some very shady things. And that poor wife of his, *she* looks pretty downtrodden. I wouldn't be at all surprised if he had some little popsy tucked away somewhere, he's just the type— I say!' she said excitedly. 'You don't think that there was anything between *Lee* and him ...'

I stared at her. 'Of course! I'm sure you're right. That would explain all sorts of things ...'

'Do you think Charles knew?'

I thought about Charles's trip to London in January.

'I wonder.'

I put some more water in the teapot and stirred it energetically.

'I'm going to meet him on Friday,' I said. 'Anthea's asked me to dinner and he's going to be there. I must say, I'm longing to see what he's actually like!'

'I didn't know Anthea and Ronnie knew him.'

'Rotary, I gather. And Anthea said they owed him hospitality . . . '

'Ronnie had better look out, accountants can't be too careful who they associate with.'

'Oh, I don't think it's actually business. Anyway, I'll be able to see him and judge for myself, and, who knows, I might be able to ferret something out about Lee. I don't think the police have enough evidence against anyone to do anything definite before the inquest.'

'Oh, the inquest! I hadn't really thought about that. You'll have to give evidence, I suppose. Oh, poor Sheila, it will be awful for you. When is it? Jack and I will come with you, of course . . . '

'Bless you, that would be a comfort. I must say I am rather dreading it. I'm trying to put it out of my mind until it actually happens.'

'Have you got a hat?'

'Yes, I thought I'd wear my black funeral one, you know . . . '

'Oh yes, good idea. I suppose Jamie will be there. I expect he's the only next of kin she's got. It will be fascinating to see him. You know, I really can't bear to think that he killed Lee. Do try and find out something about the horrible Bradford man. I wouldn't mind it being *him* at all.'

Chapter Twelve

I arrived at Anthea's dinner party just after seven o'clock to find that Philip Bradford was already there. He had a glass of whisky in his hand and it didn't look like his first. Ronnie was always very generous with his drinks.

'Come on in, Sheila. Nice to see you. G and T isn't it?'

'Just a small one please, Ronnie, not one of your super-specials if I've got to drive myself home!'

'Righty-ho. Now, do you know Philip? Philip, have you met our old friend Sheila Malory?'

Philip Bradford gave me a slightly puzzled look.

'I don't believe I've had the pleasure,' he said uncertainly.

It was plain that he had a vague memory of my face, but he couldn't quite place me. I hoped that my appearance was quite different from that time when we had met by the lift in Lee's apartment block. Indeed, I'd made a special effort for this evening. I was wearing my black velvet skirt and white lace evening blouse (almost a uniform for Taviscombe dinner parties) and had put on some eye-shadow and even had my hair blow-dried into a different and, I hoped, more fashionable style.

'No, we've never met,' I said, 'though of course,'

I added irrelevantly, 'I've seen your photo in the *Echo* quite often. It was in last week, wasn't it? You must be very busy with all that council work.'

He preened himself – he really was a thoroughly objectionable man.

'Yes, that's right. Service to the community – and doesn't do *me* any harm, if you know what I mean!'

I gave a little laugh. 'Oh well, why not?'

He sat down in the chair beside me. He was the kind of man I really dislike, the kind who leans confidentially and puts his hand on your arm whenever he wants to make a point. He obviously fancied himself as a ladies' man and I wondered how I was going to get through the evening without a feeling of nausea. I don't mind old–world gallantry, like old Mr Welsh at the Stroke Club who bows from the waist and calls all the helpers 'dear lady', but this kind of slimy (Rosemary was right) attention was quite different, since it sprang not from a natural courtesy, but from the man Bradford's perception of himself as a charmer.

He embarked on a long story of how he had helped to rehouse an elderly couple who had suddenly found themselves homeless. It was very complicated and designed solely to show what a splendid and generous-hearted person Philip Bradford was. I sat there wide-eyed, saying, 'Did you *really*, how marvellous!' at intervals. This seemed to be sufficient to keep him going because he embarked on a second story, this time to illustrate his brilliant business acumen and sharp commercial mind. My face was beginning to set in a dreadful false smile when Anthea mercifully shepherded us in to dinner.

I noticed that she obviously thought Philip Brad-ford was an important guest, because she was using her best dinner service and we had a fish course as well as the smoked salmon pâté and the Stroganoff. Like Rosemary, I hoped that Ronnie hadn't got his eye on a business connection with Bradford.

'When's Moira coming back?' Anthea asked him.

He seemed a little put out by the reference to his wife, but answered easily enough, 'Oh, in about ten days' time. They haven't arranged the flight yet.'

'And how do you fancy being a grandfather?' she persisted. I couldn't help smiling at his distinct displeasure at this image of himself.

'Oh, how *lovely*,' I gushed. 'I *long* for grand-children.'

Automatically on cue, as I knew he would, he said, 'Oh, but you're *far* too young to be a grand-mother!'

With difficulty I managed a simper. 'Oh, Mr Bradford! How sweet!'

'Not Mr Bradford – Philip.'

The conversation flowed back and forth along the usual lines – the weather (cold but seasonable), the number of unemployed in the town (young lay-abouts who don't want to work), the new repairs to the harbour wall (necessary for the tourist trade, but should have government funding not soak the poor old tax-payer) – and I didn't see any oppor-tunity to pop in a question that might connect up with Lee.

Then Anthea said, 'Oh, talking of tourists, Philip. Are you still renting out that holiday cottage?'

'Oh, have you a cottage?' I asked. 'What a mar-vellous investment! Where is it?'

'Oh, it's very remote,' said Anthea, answering for him. 'Miles away in the middle of the moor, just outside Brendon.'

I couldn't believe my luck. 'Which side of Brendon?' I asked.

'The Taviscombe side. It's about a mile from the village. People seem to like to get right away on holiday, back to nature and all that. I never have any trouble letting it. Booked up all the summer and right on into late October last year.'

A little more probing and I had a pretty clear idea where the cottage was. It was less than a mile from Plover's Barrow.

'I should think it's a bit of a headache in the winter,' I said. 'I mean, I expect you have to keep an eye on things, to see that it doesn't get frozen up – burst pipes and all that.'

'Yes, it's a nuisance sometimes, but I get over there most weeks.'

I wondered if he had been there on the day that Lee was murdered, and decided to do a bit more fishing and mentioned the inquest, trying to sound suitably nervous and fluttery. Bradford seemed rather anxious about the idea of an inquest. I suppose he was afraid of what might come out about his business dealings. We talked around the subject of Lee's death for a while and then, to my delight, Anthea asked Bradford, 'Did you ever meet her, Philip?'

Again, there was a certain edge of unease.

'Yes, as a matter of fact I did. I bought the cottage through her firm.'

Sensible, I thought, to admit something that could be checked.

'We didn't like her, did we, Ronnie? Not at all

135

the type of person that Charles would ever have been happy with.'

'Charles?'

'Our friend Charles Richardson – did you ever know him? No, well, he left Taviscombe quite a long time ago, probably before you came here. They were going to be married.'

I had the impression that Charles's name was not unknown to him, but he still seemed very much taken aback. His smooth manner vanished and he asked sharply, 'When was all this arranged?'

'Well, Charles was over here just before Christmas, and then *she* went over there – that's right isn't it, Sheila? And they arranged everything then.'

He made no comment but sat there, obviously thinking furiously. Anthea appeared not to notice and went on.

'*We* never thought that she was a suitable person for Charles. Well, he had that first unfortunate marriage – those poor little children – he doesn't seem to have much sense when it comes to women!'

I dropped another stone into the pool.

'But you must admit that she was very attractive. Didn't you think so, Mr Bradford – Philip?'

He hesitated, and then the smooth manner returned and he said, 'Oh, quite a charmer – a pleasure to do business with a charming lady!'

I had the impression that he wanted to make further enquiries about Charles but didn't want to seem too interested.

'Did you say that he – this man – lives in America? Were they going to live there?' he asked.

'Well,' Anthea replied, 'Charles said that he wanted to come back and live in England, but I don't know.'

'He'd find it pretty small beer after gadding all over the world for that firm of his,' Ronnie said. 'Martenco – petro-chemicals,' he explained. Bradford looked very thoughtful.

'A multi-national?'

'Oh yes,' I said enthusiastically, 'very high-powered. Charles was very much the local boy who made good, you know. Frightfully rich.'

Anthea got up and fetched the puddings from the trolley.

'Now then,' she said, 'raspberry Pavlova or lemon mousse?'

I made those exclamations of delight and admiration that all women make when confronted by the fruits of long and complicated culinary labour on the part of their hostess, and chose the lemon mousse. I had a sudden idea and turned to Bradford.

'I've just thought, Philip,' I said. 'Your cottage sounds just what some friends of mine are looking for to stay in for the Easter holidays.'

'What friends?' Anthea asked with interest.

'Freda Benson – do you remember her? She went to teach modern languages at a school in Sheffield. She wants to come down with a couple of friends. They're mad about bird-watching,' I invented, hoping that Anthea wouldn't remember Freda Benson. Fortunately she was occupied with a recalcitrant portion of Pavlova that was in danger of shooting off the serving dish, and wasn't really listening. I turned and gazed earnestly at Bradford.

'That's why it sounds so ideal. Right in the middle of nowhere – masses of birds and the moors all round. They'd *love* it!'

'I'm not sure about Easter— '

'Oh, it doesn't have to be actually *over* Easter,'

I said hastily. 'You know what marvellously long holidays school-teachers have.'

'Well, yes, that would be all right I should think.'

'Do you have anyone to pop in to do a bit of cleaning and get some milk and things in?' I asked.

'There's a very good woman in the village who comes in a few days a week.'

'That sounds wonderful. I'd like to have a look at it before I write to Freda. Would that be all right?'

He hesitated again.

'I'm not quite sure when I can manage a day to take you over there.'

That was not at all what I had in mind. What I wanted was to have a good old poke around on my own.

'Oh, *that's* all right. I'm sure I'll be able to find it perfectly well. If you can let me have the keys I could pop in one day next week. That is,' I continued archly, 'if you *trust* me with them!'

I looked up at him ingenuously from under my eyelashes. I was glad that Rosemary wasn't there or I would have giggled and spoiled everything. Anthea and Ronnie, who were never very perceptive, seemed to notice nothing odd in my behaviour.

'Well . . . ' he said doubtfully.

'I'll be *very* careful to lock up properly. I'm frightfully conscientious, you ask Anthea!'

His naturally grasping nature finally overcame his caution, and he appeared to decide that a good spring let for the cottage was not to be missed.

'As a matter of fact,' he said, 'I've got a set of keys for the cottage on me. You'd better take them now and let me have them back when you've had a look.'

138

I burst forth into a flood of gratitude and enthusiasm on the behalf of the mythical bird-watchers.

'Tell you what,' he said confidentially, 'drop the keys in one evening and we'll have a drink on it!'

I shuddered inwardly at the thought of a drink *à deux* with Philip Bradford, but I smiled happily at him and said that it would be *lovely* and that I would look forward to it *immensely*.

'I'll just give you my address,' he said, 'and the name and address of the woman in the village who looks after the cottage ... There you are.' He scribbled on the back of a business card and handed it to me. I saw that he owned a firm of builders' merchants and thought how handy that would be for any development scheme.

'Thank you *so* much,' I said, putting it away in my handbag. 'I'll be in touch in the next few days.'

As soon as I decently could, I made my farewells, pleading the need to give Tris a run before his bedtime.

'Oh, you and your animals!' Anthea said. 'You let them rule your life!'

No animal had ever been allowed into her immaculate home, and whenever she came to see me she always brushed (real or imaginary) animal hairs from the cushions and stared disapprovingly at the threads drawn from my furniture by sharp Siamese claws.

'Thank you for a *super* evening, Anthea, Ronnie. Delicious food, such a treat. Goodbye Philip – so lovely to have met you at last ... '

Anthea and Ronnie embraced me, and I firmly held out my hand to Bradford who had shown an inclination to do the same.

I got into my car and heaved a great sigh of relief at being on my own again. Anthea and Ronnie were old friends but a little of them went a long way. As for Bradford . . . I wriggled my shoulders inside my coat as if I could shake off the slimy feeling I still had from contact with him. Had he really been Lee's lover? How *could* she!

But that was a naïve way of looking at things. I knew now that for Lee sex was just one more way of getting what she wanted in life and, I suppose, it *had* got her quite a way. I felt revolted and saddened and, perhaps thanks to the gin and Ronnie's good burgundy, rather confused.

'But right is right and wrong is wrong,' I said aloud as I turned into my drive. It might well be that Lee's false values had finally been what had caused her death. Like Rosemary, I wouldn't be at all sorry if Philip Bradford turned out to be the murderer.

Tris had heard the car and was barking excitedly as I let myself into the house, and then there was a thump followed by a wail, which indicated that Foss had just jumped down from the top of my wardrobe and was ready for supper. In spite of all the food and drink, what I wanted most of all was a nice cup of cocoa. I let Tris out into the garden to bark at the hedgehogs and put the milk on. I felt rather pleased with myself. On Monday – no, bother, not Monday because I had a committee meeting – on *Tuesday* I would go and see Bradford's cottage. I got out Peter's Ordnance Survey map of the area and found where I thought it must be. There was a track marked, round the wood, that brought one out at the back of Plover's Barrow. He could easily have got there on foot – or perhaps he went with

Lee in the car, killed her and walked back to the cottage and picked up his own car there. I couldn't think it all out logically, not times and distances and everything, but it seemed a possibility at any rate. And if I could have a good look round the cottage, who knew what I might find?

Chapter Thirteen

Tuesday was a lovely day with a bright blue sky, and in the car out of the wind there was real warmth in the sun. There were quite a few early lambs in the fields and I felt that the year was on the turn at last. Since it was such a nice day I didn't take the coast road but drove over the hill and across the moor. There was still a little snow on the higher ground but the road was clear and dry. I saw very little traffic and it didn't seem to be a hunting day. As always when I was up on the moor, my spirits rose and I even sang a little – an indulgence of which I am rather ashamed and would never admit to.

After a while I stopped and looked at the map and tried to get my bearings. More by luck than judgement I found the cottage quite easily. It lay back from the road a bit, but there was a farm gate with the name painted on it: 'Barleymead'. I stopped and opened the gate and drove up to the front door. It was a well-kept, smooth-surfaced drive – I suppose Bradford had it done at cost, like the decorations to the cottage, which was immaculate. It had a tiled roof, not thatch, but in every other respect was exactly what a summer visitor would expect a country cottage to be – white walls, and a heavy, dark, wood front door with a lot of genuine wrought-iron hinges and latches. There was even an evergreen honeysuckle climbing round the porch. I took a bet with myself that there would be an old bread oven. There was plenty of room to park at the front so I left the car there and let myself into the cottage.

The inside was even more perfect. There were heavy oak beams and an enormous old open fireplace (with a bread oven), and the staircase went straight up through a door in the sitting room. There were two rooms downstairs as well as a beautiful modern kitchen, and to my surprise the whole thing was furnished with some very nice pieces. Either Mrs Bradford had very good taste (but then how could she have married Philip Bradford?) or else he had had it all done by a firm of interior decorators. Certainly he would be able to charge a very high rent for it. It must be a nice little investment.

I don't know what I expected to find. Something that would prove that Lee had been there on the day before she died – a hairpin, perhaps, or one of those clues that featured in the more old-fashioned detective stories. But no one used hairpins now, and certainly Lee didn't; her hair was short and naturally curly. Still, inspired by that thought, I opened the door in the sitting room and went up the narrow stairs.

There were three bedrooms (one of them minute, for a child, I supposed) and a very luxurious bathroom (palest blue and white and I coveted it greatly). The bedrooms were very Laura Ashley, with pretty, spriggy printed curtains and covers. I went into the larger bedroom, which was the one with the double bed, and looked about me. Everything was neat and apparently untouched. I had hardly expected to find a rumpled, unmade bed, it is true, but I must admit that I felt slightly let down and disappointed. I opened the door of the wardrobe, but apart from a collection of wooden hangers it was empty. So were all the drawers of a rather nice mahogany bow-fronted chest and those of the old-fashioned dressing table. I sat down on the dressing-table stool and stared at my reflection in the mirror. I looked rather dishevelled and windblown and my lipstick had got eaten off as usual. I got out my lipstick and put some more on and then laid it down on the dressing table to fish in my bag for a comb. The old uneven floor had made the surface of the dressing table slope, and my lipstick rolled off and on to the carpet. I exclaimed in annoyance and bent down to look for it. At first I couldn't see it anywhere, and then, when I had got down on my knees and looked more closely, I saw that it had rolled over and come to rest against the skirting. As I went to pick it up, I saw that something else had rolled down the same sloping bit of floor. Hidden between the skirting and the leg of the dressing table was an eye-liner.

I picked it up and took it over to the window to look at it properly in the light. It was an expensive one, an Elizabeth Arden, and instead of the usual black or brown, it was navy. I was immediately convinced that it belonged to Lee. She used Elizabeth Arden cosmetics, I was sure, because I remembered recognising the smell of Blue Grass when we were in the close confines of the car together. It is a perfume that has upsetting memories for me, so I always notice it. And her eyes were so very blue that she would be sure to use a navy liner to emphasise them – I remembered all those beauty hints in *Vogue*. The fact that it was an eye-liner suggested that she *had* stayed the night. Lee looked to me like the sort of woman who put her make-up on very carefully in the morning and then didn't touch it all day except to renew her lipstick. Perhaps she'd been in a hurry that morning and hadn't noticed that the liner had rolled off the dressing table. And then I thought, my excitement mounting, if it if was the morning she had been killed, she would have been dead before she realised that it was missing, so she wouldn't have mentioned the loss to Bradford (I was sure they were very careful to leave no traces here) or come back to look for it herself.

I tried to be practical. If it did belong to Lee then it would have her fingerprints on it so I mustn't handle it too much. There was a box of fancy tissues on the dressing table and I took a handful and wrapped the liner loosely in them, taking care not to smudge any prints that might be there. Then I put it in an empty plastic bag I found in my handbag. Peter used to groan at the immense amount of junk I carried around in my bag, but, I thought triumphantly, it *does* come in useful sometimes!

I put my lipstick away and combed my hair, smiling at myself in the mirror. Then I went downstairs. If they *had* been here, there might just be traces in the kitchen. It was unlikely that they would risk being seen eating out together, and even if they had, then I was pretty sure, from what I knew of both of them, they would have had a drink. No doubt Bradford would have tidied up to leave no trace, but, in my experience, most men never really leave a kitchen looking quite impeccable.

I looked around and was gratified to see that there was a trace of spillage in the smaller oven of the elegant electric stove. It was still quite soft and hadn't been burnt on, so it wasn't a relic of previous visitors. And it was obvious enough for a housewifely eye to spot it, so it must have been done since Mrs Ellis – the woman in the village – had last come in to clean the cottage. I imagined that they had brought some sort of made-up dish in a foil container and heated it up. I found myself wondering what it had been.

Inspired by this discovery, I looked in the pedal bin, but that was empty and lined with a clean plastic dustbin bag. This evidence of Mrs Ellis's zeal reinforced my belief that she would certainly have cleaned the oven properly. I poked around the kitchen a bit more, opening cupboards, and admiring the high standard of equipment. I even found myself regretting that Freda Benson wasn't coming at Easter, since I would have had no hesitation in recommending the cottage. The refrigerator was switched off, but when I opened the small freezing compartment there was still water in the ice-cube tray. Mrs Ellis, I told myself, would have made sure it was empty before she defrosted the fridge, so Bradford had probably switched it on to make ice for their drinks.

I was really very pleased with myself as I let myself out of the cottage, carefully double-locking the door behind me. I sat in the car and took stock of what I had found out. Lee had certainly spent at least one night there, though there was no way I could prove that it was the night before she was killed. Still, I felt I had established a personal connection between her and Bradford. Whether that gave him a reason for killing her I didn't know, but it was a start. Anyway, since I had a perfect excuse, it would do no harm to have a word with Mrs Ellis. I drove on into the village and found her bungalow in the main street. It was, as I would have expected, immaculately kept, with a blue front door and a plethora of net curtains. I rang the bell, and a young woman came to the door with a small girl clinging to her hand. I was surprised, since I had imagined somehow that Mrs Ellis would be an elderly 'treasure'.

I explained who I was and that Mr Bradford had said that she looked after the cottage, and would she mind turning on the electric heaters and getting in milk and bread for my friends if they decided to come at Easter.

'Come in, won't you?' she said, and I followed her into a small sitting room, brightly papered and crammed with innumerable small objects. A little boy of about two was playing with bricks on the floor, and I marvelled that all the bric-à-brac was intact, remembering Michael's destructive tendencies at that age. However, it seemed that Mrs Ellis's children were as impeccable as her house, and the boy went on playing peacefully and the little girl, who was a few years older, sat quietly on the sofa watching the television which was showing an episode of an Australian soap opera.

'Half a mo,' Mrs Ellis said, 'I'll just turn this thing down.'

She turned the sound down, but the child still sat regarding the now silent screen with its bright images of sun-drenched beaches and patios.

'That's better, now we can hear ourselves think!'

I repeated my request on behalf of my friends.

'Oh yes, just let me know when they'll be coming. I'll have given the place a good going over, of course, but I can see to the bread and milk and anything else they want. Barry might have some early lettuce by then and I could make them an apple tart . . . '

I regretted more than ever that this pearl among holiday cottages would not be occupied by Freda and her friends.

'That would be absolutely marvellous. I'll let you know the dates as soon as I hear from them.'

'Would you like a cup of coffee?'

I realised that Mrs Ellis was probably lonely, as young housewives with small children so often are, and would welcome a chat.

'That *is* kind, I'd love one.'

She went out of the room and I asked the little girl what her name was.

'I'm Debbie, and he' – she indicated her brother – 'is Craig. But *he's* not two yet.'

I trotted out the second classic gambit. 'And do you go to school?'

'Yes, but I broke my leg falling off my new bike. They put it in plaster, but now they took it off and I mustn't run about, just sit quiet.'

Her eyes returned to the television screen where the soap opera had been replaced by the vaguely familiar face of a politician in relentless close-up. Mrs Ellis came back with two mugs of coffee and a plate of custard cream biscuits. I took the coffee gratefully but declined the biscuits. She gave each child a biscuit, which they ate silently and neatly. I began to have considerable respect for Mrs Ellis.

'Debbie tells me she broke her leg.' I said.

'Yes. It was that new bike she had for her birth-day. I said it was too big for her but Barry would have it that she'd grow into it. Men!'

I smiled sympathetically. 'It seems to have mended quite well.'

'They say it has at the hospital. But it means she's off school for all this time . . .'

'Are there many children in the village?'

'No. We're the only family now with young children. Mostly old people, retired and such-like, and holiday homes, people only here at weekends. Hardly seems worth the school bus coming all this way just for one. It'll be better when Craig starts.'

'I suppose there's no way you can get him to a play-group or anything.'

'No – there's nothing like that nearer than Taviscombe. Seems a shame somehow. I'd like to move, but Barry's lived here all his life, works on the farm just down from the village. He's a cowman. *He* won't move. Still, I made him get a mortgage so's we could buy this place. I wasn't going to live in a tied cottage like his Mum and Dad . . .'

'You're not from round here, then?'

'No, from Taviscombe. My Dad's a milkman. Shapwick, his name is, Fred Shapwick.'

'No!' I exclaimed. 'He used to be my milkman. Right up until last year when his round was changed! You must be Maureen!'

'Mrs Malory! I thought the name was familiar when you said it . . . Dad often talked about you and your husband. He gave Dad some very good advice once when he got into trouble over some HP.'

We smiled at each other in genuine pleasure, as one does when life presents one with these neat coincidences.

'Well,' I said, '*isn't* it a small world!'

In recognition of this truth, she passed me the

plate of biscuits again and this time I took one.

'It's a good-sized bungalow,' I said, 'and you've got it looking so nice. But then, when I think how beautifully you've kept Mr Bradford's cottage, I'm not surprised.'

'To tell you the truth, I'm glad of something to do. You can get round this place in a couple of hours and when Debbie's at school there's only Craig to see to. And I like looking after nice things.'

'Yes, the cottage is very nicely furnished, isn't it.'

'He had it all done, by some firm. He doesn't know anything about antiques and things and I've never seen his wife. She doesn't have anything to do with the letting.'

I had the feeling that she didn't like Philip Bradford, despised him, even. Probably he had tried to patronise her, and that would have been a mistake.

'I don't expect he has any trouble in letting it. It really is a lovely spot and the cottage looks most comfortable.'

'Charges the earth for it. But then, people like that from London, they'll pay anything for somewhere in the country. Me, I'd rather go where there's a bit of sun!'

'Was it booked up all last year?'

'Oh yes, every week practically. Except when he used it himself.'

'He stays there himself?'

'Yes, sometimes.' She hesitated, but the urge to impart a little gossip was irresistible. 'A love nest, you might say.'

I guessed that the Ellis's took one of the more lurid Sunday papers.

'No!' I exclaimed.

'I'm not supposed to know, of course,' she said. 'He tries to tidy up himself when he's been. But you can always tell.'

'Wash-basins,' I said wisely.

She gave me an approving look. 'Men seem to think that taps just clean themselves,' she said. 'Oh, lots of little things *they* wouldn't notice.' Mrs Ellis seemed to have no very high opinion of men.

I took a deep breath. There was something I very much wanted to ask. I hoped that we were now on sufficiently cosy terms to do so.

'Do you ever see the women? I mean, are there several or just the one?'

She drew her lips into a thin line of disapproval. An old-fashioned young woman, Mrs Ellis, but I could have guessed that, I suppose, from her children.

'There used to be several, but lately, these last few months, there's been just the one.'

'Really! Much younger than him?'

'No, not really. I was quite surprised – the others were girls, from his office I should think. No, this one's older, in her forties, but very smart. She's got very good clothes, you know, casual but very good quality, suede and that.'

'Sounds very sophisticated,' I said, 'not really his type I'd have thought.'

'That's right. Treats him very off-hand, she does, and he loves it. I saw them sometimes, when the weather was nice, out in the garden. The cottage is down in a dip, but if you're walking along the back road you can look down and see it quite clearly. I don't suppose he'd know that. Shouldn't think he's walked anywhere in his life!'

151

'Did – do they meet here or come separately?'

'Oh, she always comes in her own car – a dark green one it is, big, must be expensive. She must have money – I can't think what she sees in him!'

'I don't suppose she comes in the winter, though, does she?'

'She didn't come for quite a bit, and then, in the New Year, she was here for one night.'

'In the New Year?' I asked, hardly daring to breathe.

'Yes, the first Tuesday, that would be. I know because I saw her car drive through the village in the afternoon and then I saw it at the cottage early the next morning.'

'Really?'

'Yes, well, it was quite a coincidence, really. I had to take Debbie here to the hospital to have her plaster off and the ambulance was calling at half past eight – it has to come ever so early so they can pick up people on the way in. Barry's mum was having Craig for me – well, toddlers get so fed up hanging about in hospitals, don't they – so I took him round just before eight. She lives up on that back road, so I looked down at the cottage as I went by and saw the car was still there. It was ever such a cold day and I thought they'd have to have all the heating on full blast if they were there over-night. That cottage isn't damp but it takes quite a while to warm up. It's what Barry's dad calls back-sundered, doesn't get a lot of sun till the afternoon. Anyway, she was there that night, but I haven't seen any sign of her since. P'raps she's got fed up with him, or else his wife's found out.'

'Goodness,' I said, 'it's just like a telly play!'

'Oh, we see all sorts round here,' she laughed. 'You wouldn't believe.'

I was wondering how to change the subject so that she wouldn't suspect that my only interest was Philip Bradford and his visitor, when the little boy suddenly caught sight of the plate of biscuits and grabbed at it, spilling them all on the floor. We knelt on the floor to retrieve them and Mrs Ellis said, 'Now look what you've done – what will Mrs Malory think!' and Debbie said primly, 'He shouldn't have another biscuit, it'll spoil his dinner.'

I looked at my watch gratefully and got up.

'Good gracious, is that the time! You'll be wanting to get on and give the children their dinners. I'm so sorry.'

'It's been nice having a chat,' she said. 'Just you let me know when your friends are coming and I'll see to everything.'

I was so absorbed in thoughts of Lee and Philip Bradford that for a moment I couldn't think what she meant. Then I pulled myself together and thanked her.

'And do, please, remember me very kindly to your father and tell him that I miss him.'

'I'll do that. Dad'll be ever so interested that I've seen you.'

I said goodbye to the two children and Debbie responded politely.

'They really are marvellous children,' I said, as we went to the door. 'So beautifully behaved! When I think what my son was like at that age . . . '

She looked pleased and said, 'You've got to be firm with them, else they rule your lives.'

I was amused at this echo of Anthea's remark about my animals. But we all, I thought as I went down the path to my car, need someone or something to rule our lives, or how empty they would be. Then I thought of Lee. Money and possessions had ruled her life, and look where *that* had got her.

Chapter Fourteen

I didn't feel, somehow, that I could tell Inspector Dean about my find – for all I knew, what I had done was illegal. So when I got back I telephoned Taunton police station and asked to speak to Roger.

'Sheila? Is anything the matter?'

'No, but I've got something to tell you, and something to show you. But unofficially, as it were.'

'Ah. Well now. I have a day off tomorrow and I know that Jilly wants to have a session with her mother about curtains and things for the new house, so I could drive her over to Taviscombe and, if you like, come and see you some time in the afternoon, and you could tell me then.'

'Oh marvellous, bless you, Roger. But what will you tell Rosemary and Jilly?'

'I could be borrowing a book, do you think? I could say I rang to see if you'd got a copy of – what? *Dynevor Terrace*. Have you got a lending copy of that, by the way? I've always wanted to read it and never been able to get hold of it.'

'Indeed I have. I always buy up copies of Charlotte M. Yonge whenever I see them in secondhand book-shops, so that I can lend them to fellow enthusiasts. I've got two spares of *Dynevor Terrace* so you shall have one to keep – unless that counts as bribing the police?'

Roger laughed. 'That depends on what you've got to tell me,' he said. 'But thank you very much indeed. I'd love to have it. I'll come about three o'clock then, if that's all right?'

Roger arrived promptly the following afternoon. I was glad to see that Foss and Tris took to him at once. Tris barked excitedly as if he was a long-lost friend and rolled with his paws in the air – something he doesn't do for everyone. Foss simply appropriated him. He took one look at Roger, leapt on to his lap, turned round twice and went to sleep.

'Oh goodness, Roger, I am sorry – put him down, you'll be all over cat hairs.'

'Certainly not, I wouldn't dream of disturbing him. I'm very honoured.' And he stroked him gently with one finger so that the very tip of Foss's tail twitched slightly with pleasure. I reflected that Jilly really had got a pearl among men.

'Now then, what's it all about?'

So I told him about the property deal – I implied that I'd got it all from Charles so as not to get Carol into trouble – and I sort of hinted that it was common knowledge, or at least gossip, that Philip Bradford was involved with Lee, and let him put two and two together. I explained how I'd had the luck to meet Bradford at Anthea's and managed to get the keys of the cottage.

'Oh, well done!' Roger exclaimed as if applauding some clever stroke.

I described the cottage and how near it was to Plover's Barrow and then I told him about the eye-liner.

'I'm positive it's Lee's. It's the make she uses, and her colour.'

156

I got up and took the plastic bag with the liner in it from a drawer.

'Here it is. I have a horrid feeling that it was probably illegal to take it. And perhaps I should have left it *in situ* as evidence, but I was terrified that Bradford might somehow see it and take it away. If only I'd had a camera ... '

Roger took the plastic bag carefully and laid it on a small table beside him.

'I don't imagine that Mr Bradford will claim ownership of this little item,' he said. 'But of course we don't know how long it's been there.'

So I explained my theory about Lee having stayed there the night before she was murdered, and all about the spillage in the oven and the water in the ice-tray.

'Good God!' he exclaimed. 'Detection *and* deduction! Remarkable, my dear Holmes!'

I laughed happily. '*And* there's Mrs Ellis!'

With some pride I reported my conversation with Mrs Ellis – about Lee's involvement with Bradford and the fact that her car was seen at the cottage on the morning of the murder.

'Women!' Roger said. 'They'll beat Special Branch any day! How on earth did you get all that out of her?'

'Well, it helped a bit that her father used to be my milkman ... '

Roger grinned. 'You're wasted – the whole WI mafia. You should be running the CID!'

'Anyway. Does it help? I mean, it's another suspect, isn't it, instead of Jamie and Andrew?'

'Motive?'

'Oh, money, of course. You see, if she was still stringing Bradford along – and she obviously was,

157

because she spent the night with him – he had no idea that she was buying up the property in Charles's name and was going to ditch him. But he might have found out that night – she might even have *told* him. The more I find out about her, the more I feel that she was an amazingly *destructive* sort of person, someone who'd hurt other people just to see them wince! Anyway, she might well have told him what she'd done, *and* that she was going to marry Charles, and that he couldn't do a thing about it.'

'For two reasons.'

'Yes, because she could let people know that he'd abused his position on the Council by telling her about the development, *and* she could let his wife know about their affair.'

'Neat.'

'*Well*. He would have been furious, wouldn't he, *and* worried, because she would be a danger to him. He couldn't, obviously, kill her at the cottage, but he knew that she had an appointment at Plover's Barrow that day. So after she'd left, he walked over there and – well – killed her.'

Roger looked thoughtful.

'It's possible. I still wonder about the client who never showed up, though. And the horseman who was seen riding away?'

'The hunt was out that day, remember? It could just have been a stray rider. Anyway, life is full of loose ends, if you come to think of it.'

'And he simply walked back to – what's the cottage called? – Barleymead. And then drove back to Taviscombe. Well, Mr Bradford certainly has some explaining to do. We'd better have a word with him.'

'Roger – I don't quite know how to put this. Could you manage to question him without letting him know that Mrs Ellis told me about him? Only if he's *not* guilty, then he'd be pretty annoyed with her, and she'd lose her job. And I think they need the money . . . '

'It's all right. Information received. He need never know that it was your Mrs Ellis. Or that it was you, for that matter.'

'Oh, I don't mind, he was an odious man and I certainly don't want to meet him again.' I suddenly thought of something. 'I must get those keys back to him somehow, without seeing him. That is – unless you want to go and have a look for yourself . . . '

'My dear Sheila, what *are* you suggesting? Entering private property without a search warrant!'

'No, of course not, I didn't think. I forgot for a moment that you were official! Well, I'll just drop them through his letter-box with a polite note. When will you be going to see him?'

'I think I'll leave that to Inspector Dean. As he's local he may have his own thoughts about Bradford, especially if Bradford has a bit of a reputation.'

'But won't the Inspector think it's odd that I told you and not him?'

'Leave it to me. Inspector Dean is an old friend and I think I can put it tactfully.'

'Oh good, I was a bit worried about that. Can you stay for some tea or will Rosemary be expecting you back?'

'No, I must get back to them, thank you very much.'

'In that case I'll get you that book. Come and have a look at my collection.'

I gave him the copy of *Dynevor Terrace* and we

had a most agreeable conversation about the linked novels, so much so that I quite forgot that he was a detective inspector until he said, as he was getting ready to go, 'I mustn't forget to take the evidence with me,' and picked up the plastic bag.

'Let me know what happens, if you can,' I said.

'I'll do my best. And thank you – for everything.'

After he had gone, while it was still in my mind, I wrote a hasty note to Bradford, saying that I thought the cottage was delightful and that I would be writing to my friends. I put the keys in the envelope with the note and got out the car. I hoped that I could drop them through his letter-box before he returned home in the evening.

He lived in a large house on the other side of Taviscombe and, as I parked outside, I was glad to see no car or any other sign of life. I thrust the envelope through the letter-box and almost ran down the path, since I really didn't feel I could bear to come face to face with Philip Bradford after all I had told Roger about him that afternoon.

That evening Michael telephoned from Oxford to ask me to send some books on to him. When I went up to his room I was appalled to see how awful it looked. Because of my obsession with the Lee affair I had neglected my household tasks. No, that's not quite true. I loathe housework and am delighted to find any excuse to turn my back on it. I needed to feel very strong, anyway, before tackling Michael's room because he never, ever puts anything away, and since he never throws anything away either the room was silted up with archaeological layers going right back to his early childhood. Indeed, as I looked along the overflowing shelves for Prescott's

Conquest of Mexico and *Constitutional Conflicts of the XVIIth Century*, I found scribbled-on copies of *My First Dinosaur Book* next to *Fear and Loathing in Las Vegas*.

I hadn't touched anything since Michael had gone back after Christmas, apart from throwing all the inferior garments that he had rejected as unworthy of Oxford into the laundry basket. The room looked not only chaotic but shabby as well, and I decided that I would have it redecorated before he came back for the Easter vacation. Since I am absolutely useless with a paint-brush I knew I'd have to get it done professionally, and I seemed to remember that Marjorie Fraser had told me that she had found a very reliable man to do some decorating for her. On an impulse I rang her. She provided the name of the decorator most efficiently and then she said, rather gruffly, 'You seem to be in with the police – have they found out any more about this Lee Montgomery business?'

I guessed that she was worrying about Jamie, and felt sorry for her.

'As a matter of fact,' I said, 'I think there is something new. It's just possible that there might be someone else – other than Jamie or Andrew, you know— '

'Who is it?' she demanded.

But I didn't feel I could tell her anything about Bradford so I simply said vaguely, 'Well, I don't know for sure, but I sort of got the impression that the police have their eye on someone else. I don't know the details but I hope it might divert their attention from Jamie . . . Have you seen him recently?'

'No. He hasn't been out the last couple of times.

161

Too worried, I suppose. I spoke to him on the telephone and he said that inspector had been there pestering them. He's extremely worried about the effect of it all on Andrew.'

'Poor boy— '

'The police have absolutely no proof,' she said fiercely. 'They can't do anything if they've no proof . . .'

She sounded strained and uncertain, quite unlike the brisk, confident person I was used to. I was very sorry for her. Love is never easy, and when it comes late in life and to such an unlikely person – well, as they say, it's the devil and all.

I said, rather helplessly, 'Don't worry, I'm sure it'll all come right in the end.' But as I put the telephone down I thought that even if Bradford had killed Lee, and Jamie and Andrew were safe from suspicion, I could see no happy ending for Marjorie where the Hertfords were concerned.

Chapter Fifteen

A few days went by and I was still waiting for a word from Roger. I employed the time by catching up on my marmalade making. I had bought the Seville oranges quite a while ago and they had been sitting in the larder reproaching me ever since. Normally I had the whole thing done and the pots neatly labelled and in the store-cupboard before the end of January. As I cut up the oranges I went over and over in my mind all the events of the past weeks and I decided that, in a way, the most peculiar feature was Charles's reaction to the whole affair. He had seemed to be deeply infatuated with Lee when we all had that pub lunch together, and had sounded quite distraught when she had been missing. But oddly enough, when he actually heard about her murder, he hadn't sounded, somehow, like a lover and a fiancé. Well, of course, there were the exclamations of horror and he had certainly seemed shocked, but then there were all those questions about the police going through her papers. That, surely, had been more the reaction of someone concerned about a business deal – and a shady business deal at that – than of a man in love.

How much had he known about Philip Bradford? He obviously knew that Lee had got the tip-off about the development from someone, but had he known who? He *couldn't* have known about Lee's affair with Bradford – or could he? Would someone engaged in that kind of business deal think that an acceptable way of getting information? I pulled myself up short. What a horrible thing to think about one of my oldest friends. Next I would be wondering if *Charles* had murdered Lee!

There was, a voice inside my head whispered, the little matter of that plane ticket to London in January. I had pushed that particular piece of information to the back of my mind, preferring not to think the unthinkable, but now I took it out and examined it. If – *if* Charles was really interested in Lee only for the money she could make for him, then all he had to do was finance the property deal. Everything would be in his name and Lee would expect to get her share when they were married and Bradford had been jettisoned. But suppose Charles had been using Lee and had never intended to marry her? It would have been easy, once he knew that everything was signed and sealed, to fly over and arrange by telephone to meet her in a remote spot (easy to think of some excuse for that). Then he could have hired a car and driven to a lay-by on the coast road and walked down to the house. Charles was a local and knew his way around the moors so that would be no problem. She would have been expecting him and would have let him into the house. Perhaps *Charles* was the mysterious 'client' she was meeting there. Then, after he had killed her, he could have been in London in time to catch the late afternoon flight and be back in New York that evening, such are the marvels of modern travel! And there he would be, far away from the scene of the crime, waiting to be told that Lee was dead so that he could be a grieving fiancé.

But the body hadn't been discovered for quite a while, and he had got restless and, furthermore, he knew that he must appear to make enquiries about her – why she hadn't written or telephoned. So what would be more natural than to get in touch with his old friend Sheila, who was always so splendid, and get her to set the wheels in motion. By now the marmalade had reached the required slow, rolling boil and I stirred it agitatedly. It would all fit. I checked my thoughts. I had been speculating, moving theories around like pieces of a jigsaw puzzle, seeing if they could be put together in some way to form a picture. It was, I told myself, like playing a game. Of course Charles wasn't like that. I had known him all my life – he simply wasn't capable of doing such a thing.

But how well *do* you know him? that tiresome inner voice persisted. People we've known all our lives suddenly do the most amazing and unexpected things, especially if the motives are strong enough. And Charles's life had always been dominated by financial gain, we had all known that – Jack and Ronnie had rather admired him for it. Charles had been prepared to spend years of his life going round the world, leading a fairly nomadic existence and breaking up his marriage in the process, for the considerable financial rewards it had brought him. Would he have been prepared to go this far, to make 'a pretty good killing'?

The marmalade was setting and I took the preserving pan off the stove and put the jars to warm. I would wait and see what Roger had to say about

Bradford, I told myself. *That* was a perfectly reasonable theory and much more comfortable. If Lee had threatened him ... He would have lost a great deal of business as well as prestige if he was turned off the Council, and he was the sort of self-important man, a large fish in a small pond, who would hate to lose face, even to his wretched, long-suffering wife. Yes, a more plausible suspect altogether.

I opened the back door to let out the powerful smell of marmalade, and Foss came rushing in and leapt up on to the work surface, leaving a pattern of muddy paw-marks. As I automatically wiped the surface clean I resolved to concentrate on my own life for a bit and clear my mind of upsetting suspicions.

Roger telephoned the next afternoon.

'I'm sorry, Sheila. After all your hard work ... Dean has been to see Bradford and I'm afraid he has a perfectly good alibi for the time of the murder.'

'Can you tell me?'

'Well ... It seems that he was in a council meeting at nine thirty that morning.'

'But— '

'Yes, I know what you're going to say. But even if he had actually gone to Plover's Barrow with Lee in her car – and they hadn't left by eight, remember – he still had to kill her and then walk back to the cottage, pick up his own car and drive back to Taviscombe by nine twenty, which is when he arrived. It's simply not on. As it is, he would have had to be pretty nippy to get back to Taviscombe by then.'

'Oh dear, yes. I see. What about Lee being at the cottage?'

'He doesn't deny that. He was pretty embarrassed, of course, and hopes it won't have to come out at the inquest . . . '

'Will it?'

'Actually, we're asking for an adjournment. There'll be the absolute minimum of formalities, I expect. You'll have to be there, but I shouldn't think you'll be called.'

'So it wasn't Bradford.'

'Apparently not. Sorry about your clever detection. Not quite all in vain, though. It does help us to build up a fuller picture of Lee Montgomery.'

The name Montgomery struck a chord.

'Roger, what about his wife? Montgomery's, I mean. She had a motive, in a way.'

'Actually, we did check her. She died last year. I'm afraid you're clutching at straws a bit, aren't you.'

'I suppose I am.'

'So now we'll have to go on looking at the only suspects left to us.'

'Jamie and Andrew?'

Roger hesitated.

'Yes. Though there is someone else we might consider.'

'Who?'

'Charles Richardson.'

Now it was my turn to be silent for a moment.

'Charles!' I said at last, and tried to make it sound as if the possibility had never occurred to me. 'But he was in America!'

'There are such things as planes. Concorde, even. You could be there and back in one day at a pinch. Certainly two.'

'But Charles was going to marry Lee.'

167

'Possibly – possibly not. We've found some very interesting documents among her papers at the flat. She'd bought up property in his name which, if this development thing goes through, will be worth well over a million pounds. Perhaps he didn't want to share it with her. It's a lot of money, if money is what you care about.'

'But if everything was in his name he wouldn't *have* to kill her.'

'In a way, but she could have made things awkward for him. As it is, as far as he knew she had no next of kin, no one to make a fuss about the money anyway. I think you told me that he thought she was divorced.'

'Yes,' I said, trying to sort things out, 'he didn't know that she was still married to Jamie. I suppose *he's* her next of kin.'

'Precisely. He'll get anything she might have to leave. That will certainly come in handy. They seem to live very much from hand to mouth.'

'But Jamie thought she hadn't any money,' I said quickly. 'He told me . . . '

'That's what he told you, yes.'

I felt thoroughly miserable. Everything I thought of seemed to implicate Jamie or Charles. A million pounds! Charles could have his pick of attractive females with a million pounds. Lee was quite bright, but, in trusting Charles, had she been bright enough?

Roger said sympathetically, 'I'm sorry, Sheila, I know how distressing this must be for you. It's very hard to think of anybody one has known for ages as a possible murderer. But these things do happen, you know – have happened – and we just have to get at the truth the best way we can.'

'Yes, of course, Roger, I do see that. It's just that
... well, you know. Thank you for telling me.'

'I'll see you at the inquest, the day after tomorrow, isn't it? And then, after that, try and put it out
of your mind. Why don't you go and spend a few
days in Oxford – see your son, do a bit of reading
in the Bodleian ... '

'What a good idea, perhaps I will.'

But I knew that while this wretched thing was
unsolved it wouldn't matter where I was, it would
still worry and niggle at me and I'd find it difficult
to concentrate on anything else. I felt very depressed
about it all. I had rather meanly hoped that Bradford
would be the villain of the piece because I had disliked him, but life, as we all know, is not like that.
On the principle that if you're *really* fed up then
the best thing is to do a job you actively hate, I
decided to clear out Michael's room to get it ready
for Marjorie's Mr Owen to start decorating as soon
as possible.

As I heaved furniture about and ruthlessly thrust
ancient, yellowing copies of *Motorcycle Weekly* into
black plastic dustbin bags, I felt that there was something at the back of my mind that might explain
everything if only I could think what it was. But, as
when you try to remember the name of a small-part
actor in an old film, thinking about it simply drives
it away, and the only thing to do is to wait and see
if it'll come to the surface of its own accord. So
I turned Foss out of a cardboard box, which he
had appropriated, and began neatly packing away
Michael's old school exercise books.

Chapter Sixteen

Mr Owen was a large, middle-aged Welshman, a redundant miner who had turned to building and decorating. I wondered why he had come to Taviscombe.

'Always liked this part of the country,' he said. 'Me and the wife used to come on the steamer for day-trips. Besides,' he winked, 'does no harm to have the Bristol Channel between me and the wife's mother.' He was a good worker and marvellous at clearing up – as I suppose I might have expected of someone recommended by Marjorie Fraser – and it was a relief not to have Radio One constantly blaring away. He did ask me if I minded if he played his tapes on his cassette recorder. Of course, I said that would be fine, and waited with interest for full-throated Welsh male-voice choirs, but it turned out to be Glen Miller and Perry Como, and, after the first morning, I found myself going about my household tasks humming 'String of Pearls' and 'Catch a Falling Star', which was cheering, somehow.

I had had a note from Mr Hawkins, the vet, to say that Tris's annual booster injection was due, and, groaning inwardly, I nerved myself to take him there. Tris, normally a happy, obedient little dog, became a whining, trembling, obstinate fiend whenever we came within fifty yards of the vet's door. I hauled him into the waiting room, where he immediately went to ground under my chair and sat cowering and uttering pathetic little yelps. I tried to ignore him as I looked at the other, perfectly well-behaved animals around us – a placid labrador, lying peacefully on its owner's feet, a white poodle with a neatly bandaged paw sitting smugly on a chair next to his mistress, and a black and white cat, wrapped in a woollen shawl, on its owner's lap, who gazed at us scornfully and opened and shut its mouth in a silent miaouw of contempt. As so often happens in such places, the animals ignored each other while their owners exchanged symptoms.

' . . . cut his paw on this broken bottle. People really shouldn't be allowed . . . '

' . . . I think it's his teeth, he's *quite* an elderly gentleman now . . . '

' . . . no, only a routine injection, thank goodness . . . '

The door opened and my heart sank when Marjorie Fraser came in with her spaniel and sat down next to me. I greeted her and stroked the dog.

'Marjorie, how nice to see you – hallo Tessa; good girl! – I've been meaning to ring and tell you how delighted I am with Mr Owen. He really is a treasure!'

'Yes,' she said, 'his work is quite satisfactory.'

We chatted for a while about decorating and she told me about the extension she was planning to build and how she needed extra stabling for her horses. 'Of course, they weren't actually built as stables,' she said. 'So they will need to be extensively rebuilt. I had been thinking about finding somewhere bigger.'

'Somewhere like Plover's Barrow would have suited you,' I said, 'although it's a bit isolated. And now, of course— '

'As a matter of fact I had considered it. I saw the particulars in the window of that Montgomery woman's agency and wondered if it might do.'

'It wanted a lot doing to it, though,' I said. 'The kitchen would have needed completely modernising, for a start. That awful old sink!'

'Yes, and those stone flags would have had to come up . . . '

'And *that* costs the *earth*, I know,' I replied ruefully, 'because we had them in our present house when we first moved in and the damp underneath you wouldn't believe – we had to have a whole new damp course . . . '

'Anyway, the house would have been far too big – it's just that it's difficult to find that amount of stabling with a smaller house. I rather want to go in for a little horse-breeding. Jamie Hertford' – she looked slightly self-conscious as she mentioned his name – 'is advising me. He has been very helpful.'

Oh well done, Marjorie, I thought. That's one sure way of engaging his interest! I was about to see if I could find out if she had seen him recently when the receptionist called me in. Needless to say, I had a dreadful time hauling Tris out from under my chair, and when I did, he refused to move a step, his nails making clattering noises on the linoleum as I tried to drag him along, while the others looked at me as if I was some kind of inhuman monster. Finally, avoiding Marjorie's eye, I had to pick him up bodily and make my escape into the surgery.

'Well then, how's my old friend?' Mr Hawkins boomed cheerfully as I put Tris on the examination table and he, the little hypocrite, barked excitedly and licked Mr Hawkins lovingly on the nose. Animals!

I thought quite a bit about Marjorie and the Hertfords. She must have rather a lot of money, and if she were to go into some sort of partnership with Jamie for breeding horses . . . Jamie would benefit – and Andrew, who was so good with horses – and Marjorie would have a constant excuse to be with him, without the need for any overtly emotional sort of relationship, which would suit them both very well. It would be a splendid arrangement all round. I positively beamed with approval. Then I remembered that Jamie was the number one suspect in a murder investigation and my heart sank.

The inquest came and went. Jamie wasn't there. As Roger had said, it was a mere formality. I saw him briefly, looking official, and he gave me a slight wave and a friendly but absent smile. I longed to ask him if he had made any progress with the case, but it seemed neither the time nor the place. Jack and Rosemary had very sweetly come with me, and after it was over we went to have a drink and a sandwich at the George. We were nice and early so it was empty and we were able to get a table in the window looking out over the sea.

'There you are, girls,' Jack said, putting down our gin and tonics. 'I'll just go and see about the sandwiches.'

'Guess what!' I said. 'Marjorie Fraser's going in for horse-breeding and Jamie Hertford's advising her!'

173

'No!' Rosemary exclaimed. 'How marvellous for her! And for him, if she's putting money into it. Though I suppose he'll get any money that Lee Montgomery left – there must be a bit. That agency must fetch something and I bet she was the sort of person who had all sorts of little deals on the side.'

I preserved a tactful silence about the extent of Lee's deals because I wasn't sure how much Roger wanted known about all that. Instead I asked, 'Where does Marjorie's money come from? She seems pretty well off. That house at Bracken must have cost a fair amount – I mean, it's got quite a bit of land. And she's talking about having it extended and more stables built.'

'Marjorie Fraser's money?' asked Jack, putting down plates of sandwiches. 'Those are ham and those are roast beef. Oh, I think she got a very good price for her husband's practice. You know he was a vet, somewhere this side of Bristol, a lot of dairy farming round there, very prosperous. He died a couple of years ago, I believe, and she sold up and came out here. And I think she's pretty shrewd where investments are concerned – old Boothroyd, he's her broker too, was saying the other day that she's got a good head for business.'

'Oh wouldn't she just!' said Rosemary disgustedly. 'That woman is too perfect for anything! No wonder everybody loathes her!'

'I'm beginning to feel sorry for her, in a way. It's quite pathetic when she talks about Jamie, rather like a school-girl with her first crush!'

Rosemary snorted.

'Anyway,' I said, 'I'm grateful to her for finding Mr Owen for me . . . ' and the conversation turned exclusively to decorating, imperfectly lagged pipes and the iniquities of plumbers.

That evening I had just switched off the television after watching a particularly horrible thriller, in which every character was either revoltingly vicious or repellently weak. I feebly stayed with it to the end because I hadn't got the remote control near at hand and I didn't want to disturb Foss, who was heavily asleep on my lap. I was, therefore, feeling a little irritable at having mindlessly wasted an hour on something that had neither entertained nor informed me, and, when the telephone rang, I snatched up the receiver and snapped 'Yes?' in a very brusque way.

'Sheila?' It was Charles, obviously taken aback by my uncharacteristic greeting. I was taken aback too. Suddenly to be confronted by Charles, after the theories I had invented about him, and before I had had time to collect my thoughts, was very disconcerting.

'*Charles!*' I exclaimed. 'How lovely to hear from you.'

'How are things going? Have the police any news yet?'

'Well – not a lot,' I said hesitantly. 'Haven't they been in touch with you?'

'I don't know, really. I'm just in from Johannesburg and I haven't been back to the apartment yet. But have they made an arrest or anything? I'm sorry it's been so long since I called but we've been having a fairly hectic time over here – the Aroldson merger, I expect you've heard about it?'

Since the financial pages of the *Daily Telegraph* are so much wasteland to me, I naturally hadn't, but I made interested murmurs.

'Honestly, I seem to have been going round the world non-stop since Christmas.'

I seized the opportunity to probe a little.

'Yes, your splendid secretary told me you'd been in London early this year – I wish we could have seen you.'

'Oh *that* – now that *was* a complete balls-up,' Charles said, warming to his theme. 'Fredrikson – our head of European operations – asked me to go with him to help with the negotiations – well, I know a lot of the people involved – and we got to Heathrow on the second – think of travelling the day after New Year's Day, you can imagine what my head was like! Anyway, there was a message for us at the airport that the whole bloody shooting match had been transferred to Frankfurt! Muller, *their* vice-president, couldn't get to London. Would you believe! Absolute nonsense, of course, just a ploy – still, we had to get the next flight out to Germany. All I saw of London was that God-awful departure lounge!'

'Poor Charles!'

'Actually, I tried to phone Lee from Heathrow, but there was no reply. I suppose she was out somewhere.'

'Yes, I suppose she was.'

'Poor kid – it all seems unreal, somehow.'

'The money from that property deal isn't unreal,' I said sharply.

I could almost feel Charles's interest quicken. 'Oh, has that been sorted out then? I gathered from Lee that everything was more or less wrapped up.'

'From what the police have told me, it seems that you're likely to be a very rich man.'

'It was a neat little operation,' he replied. 'Poor

Lee, if only she were still around we could really have had fun . . . '

I was suddenly furious with Charles for his casual, uncaring attitude.

'I suppose her next of kin might have a claim,' I said, dropping a stone into the pool.

'Her what?'

'Her next of kin – her husband.'

There was a stunned silence at the other end of the line and I was glad that I was not paying for what would probably be a long and expensive telephone call.

'But she was divorced.'

'No. She'd never got around to it. Oh, she was going to, when she thought you'd marry her. But she died before anything was done.'

'But this Montgomery chap . . . '

I explained about Mr Montgomery and then about Jamie.

'I'm afraid she wasn't a very nice person, Charles. The way she tried to get that last pound of flesh out of Jamie, when she simply didn't need it – well . . . '

'Good God. Jamie Hertford! We – Jack and Ronnie and I – used to think he was the last word! I can't believe it. And she – she never mentioned anything. And' – his voice sharpened suspiciously – 'that man Bradford? What about him?'

There seemed no point in holding anything back now, so I told him about Lee's last night at Bradford's cottage.

'I'm sorry, Charles, this must be painful for you.'

But I couldn't really feel sorry for him. I knew that it was only his pride that was hurt. He would soon bounce back and there would be another marvellous girl – someone more suitable next time perhaps. But, what with all the money, I wasn't very hopeful.

'That poor chap!' Charles seemed more concerned now with thoughts of Jamie.

'Poor Jamie, indeed. You realise that he is the chief suspect, him or Andrew, his son.' I told Charles about Andrew.

'Well,' he said, and suddenly he sounded like the Charles I used to know, 'if anything does happen to Jamie Hertford, I'll certainly see that the boy is all right financially. They ought to have some of the money anyway.'

'I doubt if Jamie would take anything connected with Lee – even for Andrew's sake. They just want to be left alone.'

'Fat chance of that if he *did* murder her – not that anyone could blame him after the way she behaved. Perhaps he might get off with manslaughter. A good lawyer . . . I know just the man. I'll pay, of course. I feel sort of responsible.'

'Steady on, Charles. He hasn't been arrested yet. I don't think they've anything like enough proof – it's all circumstantial evidence.'

'Well, let me know. I'm off to Chicago tomorrow, and then to Rio, but Paula will always have a number for me.'

Dazed by all this whizzing around the world, I assured Charles that I'd keep him informed and thankfully said goodbye.

'So that's that,' I said. 'It wasn't Charles.'

Foss, who had been stalking round and round the room in the purposeful way he does when he wants to indicate that it's bed-time, stopped and looked at me in surprise.

'Oh, Foss, I'm so glad, really, that it wasn't Charles,' I said foolishly.

The next morning, just before I had to collect Mrs Aston from the Out Patients department after her physiotherapy, I crossed the road and went to have a look at Country Houses. It was all shut up and there were letters pushed through the letter-box and lying on the floor. Carol must have gone – I hoped she'd got that receptionist's job. I'd find out next week, when I went for my check-up.

I looked at the photographs of properties, still in the window. They looked dusty and forlorn. In the centre, in pride of place, I saw the particulars of Plover's Barrow and idly read through the description. 'Fine property ... two acres of land ... extensive stable block ... some modernisation necessary ... ' I stared at the photograph, as if it could tell me what had happened that morning in January. Then, quite suddenly, the picture of Lee lying on the cold, stone floor came into my mind and I found myself shaking, as I had the day I'd found her. My head swam and I had a dreadful feeling of nausea. For a moment I was afraid I was going to faint and I clung to the sill of the window. I tried to pull myself together and breathed deeply, thinking, as one does, that I mustn't make an exhibition of myself by behaving oddly. After a while I felt better and able to walk on. I crossed the road slowly and went into the hospital to collect Mrs Aston. I found her sitting in the waiting area with a martyred expression.

'I got through early,' she said, 'so I've been waiting. Freezing, it is in here, people coming and going leaving that door open. I wouldn't be surprised if

I've caught a cold, sitting in a draught all that time ... '

I held the door wide open, so that she could get her walking frame through, deeply grateful to return to normality again.

Chapter Seventeen

A train of thought is a funny thing, the way your mind hops about. Mine is worse than most — 'genuine one hundred per cent grasshopper', Peter used to say. I was making a cup of tea for Mr Owen. (He'd done Michael's room so beautifully that I'd got him to decorate the bathroom, which badly needed doing.) I was putting out some chocolate digestives on a plate and humming 'Little Brown Jug', which was what Glen Miller was playing upstairs. *That* made me suddenly remember that I had, somewhere, a large brown earthenware jug that would be just right for the enormous bunch of pussy-willow, catkins and forsythia that Rosemary had given me the day before, and which were at present reposing unworthily in a plastic bucket. I had a sort of feeling that the jug was at the back of the cupboard under the sink, in among all the unused baking trays and cake tins. I got down on my knees to have a look, and as I did so I noticed that the vinyl floor-covering round the sink unit was coming away in places and really ought to be seen to. It had been down for ages, ever since we had the kitchen remodelled when we moved in. I remembered Peter and I going into Taunton to choose it. I even remembered where we had had lunch afterwards . . .

A scrap of conversation came back to me, and the elusive thought that had been floating about in the recesses of my mind for the last few weeks came to the surface, and the two fitted together with other pieces of the puzzle, and I was suddenly sure that I knew what had happened at Plover's Barrow when Lee Montgomery was murdered.

The electric kettle was boiling, so I got up off my knees and made the tea. Only one person could answer the question I had to put, but I was not at all sure what I would do with the answer when I had got it. I gave Mr Owen his tea and admired the new tiles he was putting up behind the bath. I told him that I had to go out for a while and could he make sure that the animals were in if he left before I was back. Then I got into the car and drove out to Bracken.

It was a glorious day. The sun was shining and it seemed as if spring had really arrived at last. The banks of the narrow lane I drove along, up to Marjorie Fraser's house, were dotted with primroses and celandines, and there was a haze of green on the hawthorn hedges. Spring is my favourite time of the year and it was the sort of day when I usually feel a great lift of the spirits, but as I approached the house I was so overwhelmed by sadness and apprehension that I could hardly bring myself to get out of the car.

There was no answer when I rang the front-door bell, so I went round to the stables where I knew Marjorie was far more likely to be. She was inside, grooming one of the horses as I stood in the doorway and greeted her. When she saw that it was me she gave a strange little half-smile and invited me to sit down on a wooden kitchen chair just inside the stable.

182

'Forgive me if I go on doing this,' she said. 'What can I do for you?'

It was difficult to frame the question that I had to ask, so I decided to be as blunt as Marjorie herself would have been.

'How did you know that Plover's Barrow had a stone-flagged floor?' I asked. 'That wasn't in the particulars in Lee Montgomery's window.'

She continued smoothing the mare's coat with the brush and I watched the rhythmic, circular movements for some time and began to think that she wasn't going to answer me.

'What a little thing,' she said eventually. 'And I suppose there could be some perfectly rational explanation for it, but I've had enough. I'm not very good at lying and I don't think I can go on any longer. Have you worked it all out? The academic mind is supposed to be very thorough. Though I don't see how you could have done – nobody knows . . . '

She turned at last and gave me a sharp look of enquiry, and I stared back at her, trying to match her calm manner.

'I have what I suppose you could call a theory,' I said.

'And what is that?' She sounded so much like her old peremptory self at committee meetings that I found myself speaking in the flat, level tones that I use to read out the minutes of the previous meeting.

'It was obvious, from that remark about the stone floor, and from your tone of voice when you spoke about it, that you'd actually been to Plover's Barrow, and if it had been for some perfectly innocent reason you would certainly have said so. And there was another thing at the back of my mind: a shepherd there said that he saw someone riding away from the house about midday on the day that Lee was murdered. He thought it was a man, but he was a long way away and you're tall . . . '

Marjorie had finished grooming the horse and had taken a bridle down from a hook on the wall and was polishing the bit.

'Yes,' she said, 'I was at the house that day.'

'I suppose it was for Jamie and Andrew, wasn't it?'

'In a way.'

The spaniel, Tessa, hearing voices, came into the stable. She laid her head on my knee for a moment so that I could stroke her, and then settled down in a patch of sunlight at my feet.

'I can't really believe that Jamie killed her,' I went on, 'so it had to be Andrew. I don't know how he came to be at Plover's Barrow – perhaps Lee told him about it when she spoke to him on the phone. But I can imagine only too clearly how she teased and tormented him until, poor boy, he snatched up that knife and tried to put her out of their lives for ever. I imagine that Andrew must have left some sort of note for Jamie, who came to find him. *He* would have come in the Land Rover and left it up on the road, coming down cautiously on foot, not knowing what he would find. When he saw what had happened he'd have wanted to get Andrew away as quickly as possible – the boy must have been in a dreadful state. But there was the problem of Andrew's horse. He was obviously in no condition to ride all that way back, but Jamie didn't dare leave the horse there, while he went back for the horse-box, in case someone saw it. The only person he could trust to get it back for him was you.'

184

Marjorie gave a little laugh, and the dog lifted its head and looked at her, but she didn't say anything. I continued.

'So he put Andrew in the Land Rover and stopped at that telephone box on the coast road and phoned you. You drove over and left your car, as Jamie had done, walked down, collected the horse and rode it in easy stages back to Jamie's. Then he drove you back to your car and you went back home. Is that the way it was?'

Marjorie let the polishing rag lie idle in her hand and looked at me with a strange mixture of admiration and contempt.

'Oh Sheila,' she said, 'you really are extraordinary, you simply cannot bring yourself to believe anything bad of anybody, can you. Jamie couldn't *possibly* have killed Lee Montgomery, so it must have been Andrew – a poor boy, who didn't really know what he was doing, wasn't responsible for his own actions!'

'It wasn't Jamie?'

'No, of course it wasn't Jamie, though God knows he had reason enough.' She rubbed at the bridle again, holding it up to the light to see if she'd got all the polish off. 'It was me. I killed her.'

Her voice was flat and unemotional, but there must have been some quality in it that made the mare suddenly move nervously in its stall and toss its head, and I remembered how the horse had reared and plunged when I had told Marjorie how I had found Lee's body.

'I suppose I must explain. I knew I would have to one day soon. The burden of such a thing is very heavy. And, of course, I couldn't allow anyone else to have taken the blame for what I did.'

'But *why*?' I burst out. '*Was* it for Jamie?'

'Partly. That was why I went to see her. Jamie had told me what she had said about the money. I don't think he meant anyone to know, but he was desperate with worry about Andrew, who had gone off, as you know. I just happened to phone that evening – to see if he'd got the date of the Invitation Meet,' she continued, looking rather self-conscious, and I remembered how I, too, in the first flush of love, had always found some excuse for phoning the object of my affection.

'I'd seen the advertisement for Plover's Barrow in her window, and, as soon as I'd spoken to Jamie, I phoned her office. I just caught her as she was leaving and arranged to see her at the house the next morning, pretending that I was thinking of buying it. I didn't want anyone to know I was seeing her – well, I was sure Jamie wouldn't want it known, and nor did I, for a lot of reasons. I made the appointment for the next morning, partly because I needed to see her as soon as possible, and partly because I knew I would be out with the hunt on that part of the moor that day. I got there just after eleven, a bit late – she was getting impatient and not in a good mood anyway. I knew it was no use appealing to her better nature, so I offered her money. Not as much as she would have got from her share of the sale of the smallholding, but she could have had it at once, with no strings or bother.'

I tried to visualise the scene.

'What did she say?' I asked curiously.

'She was very offensive. She implied' – here Marjorie found difficulty in forming the words and a deep flush darkened her face – 'that I was in love with Jamie. She laughed and made some very distasteful remarks ... '

I could imagine that very well. Lee would have known just how to hurt and humiliate Marjorie, and she would have enjoyed doing it.

'Did she say she'd take the money?'

'Oh yes. She was very greedy.'

'Then, why ... '

'Why did I kill her? I still wasn't sure that she would leave Jamie and Andrew alone. She said' – Marjorie hesitated again – 'she only had to lift her little finger to get Jamie back again. I was almost sure that Jamie wouldn't, but you never know with men – she seemed to have this peculiar attraction, I can't pretend to understand it – and then he'd have been unhappier than ever.' She fell silent for a moment and then continued more in her old manner. 'I told you it was only partly Jamie. That was only the last straw. I have hated Lee Montgomery – overwhelmingly hated her – for two years now.'

'But you've only been in Taviscombe for about a year ... '

'The story goes back six years, really. You probably know I used to live just outside Bristol; my husband was a vet and I helped him in the practice. We had a daughter, Lucy ... ' For the first time, Marjorie's voice broke. 'I'm sorry, it's been so long since I spoke her name. She was a marvellous girl, everyone loved her ... Well, one day she was out on her bike when this car knocked her down. There were witnesses and the police were called and Lucy was taken to hospital. She had concussion and some abrasions. They kept her in for a couple of nights and then let her come home, and she made a good recovery. The driver of the car was a woman. She'd obviously been drinking, so the police prosecuted. When the case came up she was fined for dangerous driving and had her licence taken away for a year. A year,' she repeated. She looked at me. 'Yes, it was Lee Montgomery – Elizabeth Hertford was the name she gave in court. Well, we went on as before for four years and then suddenly Lucy collapsed and within a day she was dead. It was an aneurysm, apparently, a sort of blood clot. These things happen very suddenly and very quickly . . . ' Marjorie's voice trailed away, vaguely almost, and then she said, fiercely, 'They said that the concussion probably hadn't anything to do with it, that it would have happened anyway, but how could I believe that!'

'Oh Marjorie, how terrible for you . . . '

She seemed not to hear me, and went on painfully.

'We both adored Lucy, David and I, we'd built our entire lives around her. Without her he didn't see any point in going on – I wasn't enough, you see.' She was clasping and unclasping her hands around the bridle until the metal bit into her fingers. 'He killed himself. An overdose. I don't know, really, why I didn't do the same. I suppose it's the way I was brought up. Suicide is a sin. Murder is too. But an eye for an eye . . . and for a child.'

I thought of Michael and wondered what I would have done. And then I thought of Peter who had died too, but surrounded by love and knowing that he had left a son behind him.

'After a while, I sold up the practice and moved down here. It was a place where we'd all been happy. We used to come for riding holidays – Lucy had a marvellous pair of hands, she would have been really

188

good . . . David and I always said we'd retire down here and keep horses. It seemed, almost, something I could do for him.' She looked at me. 'Was that very foolish?'

'No,' I said quickly. 'No, I would have felt the same.'

'I'd been down here for about a month when I saw her in the town and found out that she lived and worked here. It was a dreadful shock, a horrible coincidence. I used to see her driving around in that big, powerful car . . . I never told anyone about Lucy and David. It was too private and too painful. I tried to lead a normal life. I joined things, I kept busy.' She gave me a quizzical look. 'I know you all thought that I was bossy and interfering, but all that organising and managing was what kept me sane. That, and the horses.'

'Oh Marjorie, I'm so sorry.'

'I used to feed my anger. Several times I went into that place and made enquiries about houses, just to see her and speak to her. She didn't recognise me. We never met over the case and Fraser is quite a common name, I suppose. So, you see, when all this blew up over Jamie and Andrew and I saw how she was going to ruin two more lives . . . '

The mare was restless again, and shifted in its stall. Marjorie got up, put her arm around its neck and spoke quietly and soothingly to it.

'After she had gone on about Jamie, she began to sneer at Andrew, called him half-witted and other things. So then I told her about Lucy and how she had killed her . . . '

Marjorie had turned to face me, and now she was dreadfully pale.

'Do you know, she simply didn't remember the

accident, she had totally forgotten about it ...
People sometimes say, "I don't know what came
over me" – and that's really how it feels. Something
came over me, a feeling so strong that it was almost
tangible. She'd turned away, she was picking up her
handbag to go, not bothering, not caring. I took up
that knife and killed her. I was quite calm, I *did* know
what I was doing. I knew just where to put in the
knife so that she would die instantly. I know about
these things and, as you say, I'm tall, so I could
manage exactly the right angle from above.

'I wonder, did I really go there that morning
intending to kill her? I had my alibi. It's easy to
leave the hunt for a while and then rejoin it, no
one misses you, they're too absorbed, themselves.
Everyone thinks you've simply fallen behind or
taken another line across country. I left no fingerprints – I was wearing riding gloves – and there were
no tracks because I left Satin tied up at the back. I
didn't know, of course, that someone saw me ride
away. I honestly don't know if it was in my mind
all the time ... '

She turned away and leaned her face against the
mare's neck for a moment. Then she turned and
said, almost briskly, 'I knew that this would be only
a temporary respite – time to settle things properly.
I've written a letter – it's with my solicitor. I'll take
the horses to the livery stables this morning. I want
Jamie to have them – I've left him everything – well,
there's no one else now. Actually, Sheila, would you
do something for me? Would you go and see Jamie
and try and explain to him? I can't, somehow, put
it all in a letter, and I would like him to know how
it was. I would like him to think of me, well – you
know ... '

'Yes, of course I will.'

Jamie and Andrew would be amazed and sad and grateful, but, secure at last in their little world, they would have no real idea of what they had meant to her, and perhaps that was just as well.

'I know I shouldn't ask you, but can you give me a day? I mean, I know you will have to tell the police about this conversation, but if you could give me time to leave things as they should be.'

'I have to go to that meeting in Dulverton this afternoon,' I said carefully, 'and I have an appointment with my accountant tomorrow morning . . . '

'Thank you, Sheila. There is one other thing. It's Tessa. She was Lucy's dog – just a puppy when she died – and I don't want to have her put down. Would you mind taking her? She's quite obedient and she gets on all right with that Westy of yours.'

Tears that I hadn't shed for the human actors in this drama came into my eyes, stupid, sentimental tears, but none the less real for that. I bent down and patted Tessa to give myself a moment to recover.

'Of course I will . . . '

Marjorie picked up the dog's lead, which had been lying over the stable partition, and clipped it on to its collar.

'Right, then.' Her voice was brisk and businesslike, the Marjorie I knew – or thought I knew. 'Come along, then, I'll put her in your car and then she'll know she has to go with you.'

We walked together to the car.

'What a beautiful day!' she said as we came into the sunshine.

I opened the car door and she put Tessa in the back, stroked the dog's head and shut the door.

'Marjorie . . . ' I said uncertainly.

She opened the driver's door of the car.

'Thank you for everything,' she said. 'Goodbye.'

I drove out of the gate and down the lane, between the clusters of primroses and celandines. In the back of the car the spaniel was making little whining noises.

'It's all right, Tessa,' I said. 'Everything's going to be all right.'